Things Get Weird
in
Whistlestop

©2020 Julie Carpenter

book design and layout: SpiNDec, Port Saint Lucie, FL

cover image: Carmen Jones

Published by Poetic Justice Books
Port Saint Lucie, Florida
www.poeticjusticebooks.com

ISBN: 978-1-950433-34-6

FIRST EDITION
10 9 8 7 6 5 4 3 2 1

I dedicate this book to my husband, Blake, who hounded me....errrr...encouraged me to finish the book and supported me while I wrote.

I would also like to thank all my friends at The Writers Hotel. Shanna, Scott, and Scott, and Diane for their multiple readings, kind words, and encouragement.

Also, thanks to Jeff Weddle, the first person to tell me I had actually written a story.

And, of course, to Crow, who supervises my writing from my shoulder almost every day.

Julie Carpenter

THINGS GET WEIRD IN WHISTLESTOP

Poetic Justice Books
Port Saint Lucie, Florida

contents

The Story of Ida Fox May   11
The New Car   33
A Small Haunting   43
A Cautionary Tale   63
The Bite   85
A Snake in the Grass   103
Father Dingle, Some Mice,
   and the Portal to Hell   127
The Laughing Pink Elephant   147
The Strange Disappearance
   of Edna Brown   169
The Sheriff's Tale   191
The Cat Came Back   243

Things Get Weird in Whistlestop

JULIE CARPENTER

The Story of Ida Fox May

Whistlestop, October 1929

The Honorable Clayton Silver was sitting in a rocking chair on the wide front porch of his two-story farmhouse, long since emptied of children, smoking his pipe. He was watching moonbeams press down wraiths of fog rising from the creek. The ghosts drifted lazily but the weight of moonlight prevented them rising too high. They lit up silver, realized the moon was watching them, then slunk back down the bank and swam away before trying again.

Judge Silver didn't know why he still felt compelled to come outside to smoke his pipe, no matter the weather. His wife, Annie, had been dead five years. There was no one but himself to please now, and he didn't mind the smell of stale smoke. Habit, he supposed. Tonight, his warm jacket, moonlight, and the sweet pungent smell of cherry tobacco floated a possibility of contentment. He alternately whistled a tune and smoked his pipe. Then he heard it.

At first, a low murmur from behind a copse of scrub trees down the road caught his ear. His house was set back a little. The driveway curved so he couldn't quite see the road. For a moment, the low rumble seemed friendly enough, like the sound of a farm truck from a distance or a thunderstorm grumbling off behind Knobb Mountain. The drumbeat of it ebbed and swelled on the light breeze. As the sound approached, the rhythm throbbed more furiously. There were sharper sounds...voices. The friendly rumble of the distance became prickly with detail.

Judge Silver stood up and moved to the edge of the porch, holding his pipe in one hand, waiting. In a few more minutes, he saw the crowd, a blur moving toward him through drifting fog. Piercing beams of light stabbed out of an amorphous shape and bounced back off the lazy fog. The expanding, pulsating mass came toward him rapidly.

"What in bloody Hell?" he peered out into the chilly autumn night. The autumn night didn't answer, being busy as it was making ghosts out of moonlight and fog. He squinted. No use. His glasses were sitting inside on his desk.

The dream of fog was finally torn apart by a single, pale shape sprinting in front of the mob. Judge Silver was normally a man of action, but then again, he normally had some idea what in Hell was going on. He stood there on his porch, immobile, as he tried to comprehend the scene in front of him. He searched his memory for precedent. Before his brain could react, the swarm was upon him and the lone ivory-clad figure in front made a desperate leap. His pipe fell to the porch, tobacco scattering in the light wind, and he found his arms full of...Ida Fox May.

Ida was middle-aged widow who lived at the far end of Main Street, a slender quiet woman who had occasionally been to dinner at the Silver house. Her husband, Gerald, had been a friend of Judge Silver's since grade school. They had played together on the Whistlestop Wildcats high school baseball team. The judge had always admired Ida, even found her a little enchanting, with her wild black hair, penetrating eyes, and keen intelligence. Annie had liked her as well, but she told the judge that many of the women at the church didn't take to her. Her self-possession, her bright dresses, her dark eyes and wild hair, something in the way she held herself separated her from them. She was not asked to join the Home Circle.

The poor woman was trembling against him, breathing hard. She buried her face in his woolen shoulder. He caught her up against him and felt her melt with exhaustion.

"I'm sorry," she managed to whisper in his ear, still panting. "I only meant to help."

After this mysterious pronouncement, the judge turned back to the crowd. For a few moments, the mob seemed sporting. Their prey had been cornered and they could bide their time. Murmurs settled a bit while Ida struggled to catch her breath. The judge faced them still holding Ida up from her waist. Half the town was here. He forced his eyes to cut into the darkness and he took a deep breath of chilly air. The crowd pulsed forward one last time, out of the obscurity of the foggy night and took possession of his front yard. Ida drew as far up against him as she could. Her raven black hair curled wildly around her head, and her black eyes were as wide as saucers in her face.

"Lord help us all," he said firmly and loudly so everyone could hear him, "What on God's green earth are you people up to?"

He spoke slowly and solemnly, using his most judicial voice, not because he had any idea how to drive this bus nor where it was going...he was just buying time.

Right out front was Bill Cuthbert, that pasty faced ass, and his wife, Myrna. Both were puffing hard. No surprise to see Bill there. If there was a lawsuit, Bill was involved. If someone called to notify the constable that some teenagers were petting behind the cemetery, nine times out of ten, it was Bill. It was Bill that had caused that ruckus at the church over new pews in the sanctuary. Whenever there was someone making accusations or getting upset over something that ought not to have made a speck of difference to anyone...there was Bill. And here was Bill.

The warm porch light fell close to the house. Moonlight backlit the crowd so he couldn't make out many faces. The dark knot melted into anonymity back toward the bird bath, townsfolk murmuring among themselves. Judge Silver stood up straight, still holding Ida.

"I don't know what this is about," he said sternly, "But Bill, how about if you and Myrna start by stepping back off my damn chrysanthemums. Annie planted those the year before she died. Back right up off 'em." He didn't like to swear before ladies, but Good Lord if Bill Cuthbert didn't make a man lose his head.

Bill, confused and angry, gasped out, "There's something more important goin' on here than Annie's mums." He hesitated, sucking a big breath into his belly, adding petulantly, "Your honor."

"Bill," said the judge evenly, "There's nothing in heaven and earth that you could say to me right now that couldn't be said from off top of Annie's mums. And so, help me, I will not hear another word until you move your big feet two steps back."

Bill looked around at the crowd, but no one seemed to disagree with the judge on this point. Hunting down a slight, middle-aged woman under darkness of night was one thing, but crushing Annie's mums was a step too far. Whistlestop had standards. Bill took Myrna's elbow and they moved back. He stood straight and threw his shoulders back, trying to regain his dignity. His belly popped out over his belt.

The judge strained to see the back of the shadowy crowd.

"You back there by the bird bath," he said loudly, "There had better be no one standing on the pansies either." He could feel rather than see people in the back shuffling off the pansies, or in all likelihood onto them since most of the damn fools had come running out for this nonsense with no flashlights or lanterns. Despite poor visibility, he could count at least three attendees in house slippers and pajama pants.

He noticed that Ida was still trembling, and he patted her shoulder. He peered into the crowd. "You there," he said firmly to a silhouette he thought belonged to Janice Hopkins, the mayor's wife, "Go right inside and get that old green afghan off the armchair and bring it here. And get my glasses off my desk. Scoot!"

He frowned. The shadow scooted and indeed resolved into Janice Hopkins as she came into the circle of light on the porch. Judge Silver was used to telling people what to do, and they were used to doing it. That, he figured, was the only advantage he had as he tried to sort out this mess.

"I'm so sorry about this, Clayton," Ida whispered, still catching her breath. He patted her again.

When Janice returned with an afghan, he put it around Ida's shoulders, plopped her in a rocking chair, slid his glasses up over his ears and assessed the gathered townsfolk. He thought he might have seen old Allie McCall hobbling her way up front, propelled by her malevolent curiosity. And was that Charlie Johnson, that old henhouse fox, long nose almost meeting pointy chin in a smirk, arms folded over his chest? A few ladies – he thought they were from the Home Circle at church – were standing close to the porch with their husbands, whispering to each other and shaking their heads.

"Where's Father Brown?" asked the judge, "What about Sheriff Patrick?" He scrutinized the crowd, looking for a friend or two.

Janice Hopkins raised her hand, as if she were in second grade. "Janice?" asked the Judge, with a sigh.

"They've gone on a fishing trip together," she chirped.

"I see," said Judge Silver.

He turned to look at Ida, afghan wrapped tight around her shoulders. No coat, only a soft, ivory, flannel nightgown and flat, black leather slippers, hair down for the night. She was still shivering a little in the chilly night air. The sudden impulse of the mob had taken her by surprise, he supposed.

"Whatever Bill says, I didn't mean any harm," Ida said to him.

The judge faced Bill and Myrna. Myrna was clinging to Bill's arm, both of them breathing hard. They were obviously the center of this maelstrom. She wore an overcoat, a brown wool skirt peeking underneath, sturdy boots on her stubby legs. Her hair was braided round her wide head. Bill had on his work boots and overcoat as well. She and Bill, at least, knew this was coming and had dressed in preparation.

"What's the problem, Bill?" the judge asked.

Bill Cuthbert removed himself from Myrna's grasp and cleared his throat.

"That woman right there..." he paused and turned in a full circle, nearly crushing Myrna, to give everyone the benefit of seeing him swing around and stop with his pale, stubby finger pointing at Ida, "...is a witch!"

Ida sat mute in her chair, looking at her hands. The townsfolk began to clamor. Judge Silver saw a darting black shadow streak up the side of the porch and land in her lap. Ida's old black cat. She rubbed his scruffy head, fondling his torn left ear. The cat gazed at the crowd through his sharp, lemon-yellow eyes. Calmly, he started cleaning his paws.

Ida hugged him closer to her, "Mister Wilkerson," she said to him weakly, "You shouldn't be here." She put her face on his big furry head and the judge heard her whisper, "But I sure am glad to see you." Then she sat there. Quiet.

"Alright Bill," said Judge Silver, loud enough to suppress the murmurs of the crowd, "I'll tell you what. Let me fill my pipe and we'll hash this out."

He picked up his pipe from the porch floor and felt around his coat pockets for his tobacco and a match. The majority of townsfolk were probably there to be entertained by a smaller bunch of rabble-rousers. Neither group was any help to him. Of course, anyone with the sense God gave a potted geranium was at home right now in front of a nice fire. Lord, he hated his job sometimes. It was always the idiots. He took his time lighting his pipe.

After smoke was rolling comfortably out of the bowl, he said, "Let's have it then Bill."

He leaned against a porch column. He didn't want to give the weight of formality to this bedlam.

"What makes you think Ida is a witch?" he blew out a puff of smoke and let it settle on the chrysanthemums.

Bill drew himself up and turned so that the crowd could hear him as well as the judge.

"The woman that you see before you, Ida Fox May," he swept his arm dramatically toward the porch, "That woman, at 3:55 this afternoon, turned Howard William Campbell into a bird, a kestrel, to be exact. I saw it happen."

The crowd sucked in night air and expelled it in one great gasp.

The judge was a little taken aback as he had expected something somewhat less specific. He pointed at Ida, "That woman right there...turned Howard, the grocery delivery boy, into a small hawk?" He blew out a puff of smoke. He was thinking how to respond, "Today. This afternoon at exactly 3:55. Just to clarify things."

"That is exactly what happened, your honor. Although my watch may be just a minute or two slow,"

Bill said. He patted his watch pocket then folded his arms across his chest.

The crowd clucked and murmured in response. Judge Silver thought he heard a few people laughing back towards the bird bath.

Bill cleared his throat, preparing to go on when someone yelled, "Wait! Wait! Here he is!"

People were turning around and shuffling, forming a path. He saw Howard and Ronnie Smith, owner of Barton and Smith Market, making their way through the crowd.

"Here I am! Here I am!" gasped Howard.

The judge sighed. "Is that you, Howard?" he asked, "Where are your glasses?"

The judge fixed his own glasses on his nose and peered at Howard.

"Right here!" Howard waved his thick glasses in the air.

"That does seem to be Howard," Judge Silver said, "Can we drop this now?"

"I see him," huffed Bill, "I never said he didn't get better. Doesn't mean he wasn't a kestrel. I was getting to that part."

Exasperated, the judge turned from Bill back to Howard.

"Lord, Bill, you're a sap!" someone called out from the crowd.

"Ask him! Ask him!" Bill called out, pointing at Howard, "He can tell you!"

"All right," said Judge Silver, "Howard can we just clear this up? Did Ida turn you into...I can't believe I'm asking this...into a bird?"

Howard was obviously nervous. He looked down at his shoes and shuffled his feet. He was notoriously shy. Twelve-year old Howard was an awkward kid without a lot of friends. The older boys made fun of his "coke bottle" glasses. As a grocery boy, Howard had made friends with all the animals in town. He was especially fond of Mr. Wilkerson, Ida's cat.

"It's okay, Howard," Ronnie patted him on the back, "Tell the judge what happened."

"Well," Howard began, after clearing his throat a few times, "Ida May," here he stopped and smiled at Ida, she gave him a weak smile in return, "Ida had ordered some flour, and vinegar, and maybe some cheese, and oh...sugar...I can't remember if she ordered coffee or not..."

"Howard," said the judge, gently, "Can you skip ahead to the part where Ida did or did not turn you into a hawk?"

"Okay," said Howard, "I got to her house and knocked. She didn't answer so I figure she's in the garden like usual. So I set the delivery on her porch and Mr. Wilkerson there," he stopped, pointed at the cat and waved, "Hello Mr. Wilkerson, hello ole buddy! So, Mr. Wilkerson walks to the garden gate to show me Ida's there. He's really smart."

"The cat is probably her familiar!" Bill said loudly.

"Yes," said Myrna, turning to the crowd, "That means her little helper from the Devil. Bill knows all about that stuff." She patted Bill's arm.

"Good Lord!" and "Oh dear!" said a number of the Home Circle ladies from the church. There were a few guffaws from the back.

"Now, now!" Judge Silver said, "For goodness sakes!"

Something suddenly occurred to him. He squinted at Howard, "Howard, why aren't you wearing your glasses?"

Ronnie held up his hand, "He's getting to that, your honor." He patted Howard on the back to get him going again. A good hard thump or two and Howard sputtered back to a start.

"So, anyway, I follow Mr. Wilkerson round back," said Howard, "And Ida is standing there, and she looks at me and says, 'Howard, you remember how you told me the boys make fun of you for those big old thick glasses?' and I say yes...because I did remember saying that. And she says, 'Howard, I think I can help you. I really feel like I can. Do you trust me?' And I say yes. Because I do," Howard smiled at Ida again.

"And?" said Judge Silver, "Then what?"

"Well," said Howard, "She just puts her hand out like this." Howard curved his hand toward himself and then flung it out dramatically, ending with his fingers splayed. His hand stayed this way for a moment, and Ronnie helped him ease it down.

"Okay, Howard," he said, "Tell what happened then."

"She said a word I don't remember. After that," Howard said, "I felt myself pulling up inside and shutting up small. I really did. Smaller and smaller, my skin was shrinking and wrapping me up really tight. It was kind of uncomfortable."

There were gasps from the Home Circle.

Howard waited for them to settle down and went on, "And then I was falling down and started to flutter my arms and they were wings. I remember Ida standing over me and she was a giant, and I was so small, and then she took me in her hand and kissed my head...and then...it was over. I unfolded right back out into myself. And I could see! I was a little scared and tired but being turned into a bird made me better. That's what I think. I think it was all just to make me better."

Howard paused for breath, "She said, 'It's never happened like that before. But it never happens the same.' Then she gave me some lemonade and a sugar cookie and I got my delivery wagon and went back to the store."

For a moment there was silence, then the judge heard a chorus of "Oh Lord!" "Sweet Jesus" and "Lord God Help!" from the Home Circle. From the wags in the back, he heard more laughter.

"Aww...for goodness sakes!" someone called out, "C'mon Bill! Did you put Howard up to this?"

Bill was yelling, "I told you I saw the whole thing! I didn't tell Howard what to say! I can't help what I can see through my fence."

"Bill you're an ass!" said a tall shadow of a man from the gloom by the creek bed.

"He's a pompous fool!" came a woman's voice.

"He's got a point!" yelled old Charlie Jenkins, "I've seen her out late in the moonlight, a pickin' herbs!"

"I've seen her with a raven on her shoulder, feeding it bread!" Allie McCall piped out, "And I heard she gave that Edelson girl a love charm."

"She healed Emily Jo Baker's back with one word!" someone else yelled.

The judge was silent, listening to the crowd bicker with itself about Ida. He bit his upper lip with his bottom teeth, the way he did when he was thinking. He wiped his glasses.

"Howard," he finally asked, waving the crowd quiet, "Are you really telling me that Ida Fox May, this woman here turned you..." here he hesitated with distaste at his own question, "into a kestrel?"

"Maybe," said Howard earnestly, "Honestly, it was so quick, and I was so small and all...it could have been a newt or a mouse or something...but I'm sure I felt wings," he flapped his arms. He squinted thoughtfully as he pushed his glasses onto his nose and then removed them in confusion.

"Did anyone ask you to say this, Howard?" the judge asked.

"No!" Howard said, "No!"

"Did she charge anything to cure you, Howard?" asked Judge Silver.

Howard became flustered, "No. No. Of course not. Ida is my friend. She even still gave me a tip afterwards, just like always."

The crowd undulated, rippling forward to hear Howard speak again and then back from the porch where Ida sat calmly stroking her cat.

"Ha!" said Bill, "I told you what I saw. She turned him into a bird. I saw the whole thing from a knot hole in my back-yard fence."

"That's creepy, Bill," someone yelled.

"Better watch out, she'll turn you into a newt!" someone else laughed.

"This isn't the first time old Bill's been looking at women through a knothole," someone else said, "I think he's sweet on her!"

Myrna grabbed Bill by the elbow, "Bill is not sweet on an old witch!" she hollered.

Bill stood sputtering, unable to form a response.

The judge could hear the Home Circle ladies invoking the Lord Jesus. They were staring at Ida shaking their heads. Small arguments were popping up between groups of people on the lawn. The muttering was gaining in volume. No one could agree what had happened or what should be done about it.

He stared at the scene before him. The ghosts of fog still hovered at the edge of the crowd, slipping up from the creek as if to see how things would go.

The moonlight glinted off the white bird bath and fell mildly onto Charlie Johnson's tattered old dressing gown. It lit up a bit of white apron that peeked out from under Janice Hopkin's coat, and shone off Bill Cuthbert's balding head, illuminating his spider-web comb-over. Judge Silver felt he was waking into some sort of strange nightmare where dream logic was required. He turned to Ida. The porch light behind her formed a sort of halo on her wild hair. Her deep golden skin glowed in the moonlight. The shadow cat, visible only because he stained her ivory gown like ink, lay perfectly still on her thighs.

"All right everyone!" he said, turning back to the crowd. They became quiet, "I've been thinking about how to settle this thing."

He turned to Bill, "I don't know what you want me to do. Even if Ida did turn Howard into a bird, which for the record, I can't find it in myself to believe, there's no law against such a thing. Howard seems fine, and he doesn't need his glasses any more to boot. Whatever the reason is, I don't see how that's a bad thing. She's not committing fraud or even taking anyone's money. I don't know what the Sheriff would charge her with if he wanted to."

He turned to Allie and Charlie, "There's certainly no law against being out at night in the moonlight or feeding birds."

"Everyone knows there's gypsy blood in her," said Myrna, "Or worse. Just look at her!"

The Home Circle ladies had moved closer to Myrna as the night went on and they buzzed a consensus of whispers.

"She's a witch!" Bill insisted, "That ought to be enough! Nobody can do that sort of thing if they aren't partnered up with Satan! It ought to be enough that she's a witch." He crossed his arms on his chest with an air of finality.

"Well, it isn't," said Judge Silver, "There's no law against witchcraft still on the books that I know of...or as far as I know, turning someone into a bird or mouse or newt and back again. And finding a cure for someone's bad eyesight isn't necessarily witchcraft anyway. These are modern times Bill. We don't hound women over witchcraft anymore because we know better. Not that I believe any of this mess anyway. I'm half inclined to think that you're all drunk. Or I'm dreaming. Maybe Howard thought he was turned into a bird. I don't know. But there is absolutely no crime involved that I can think of."

"Now," he said, "Since no one has been hurt and everyone is accounted for...why don't we all just go home."

The crowd was uncertain for a moment. Was the entertainment over? Even the church people had to admit that Howard was certainly accounted for. A few people in the back started to drift away.

Bill stood his ground, "Ask her. Ask Ida May and see what she says! You at least have to ask her.

She's been sitting there not saying anything. That's because she did it!"

The judge shook his head. "Now," he said, "This is getting ridiculous. I won't have any more nonsense. Go home. Everyone."

But Ida Fox May stood up. Mr. Wilkerson slid to her feet, vanishing into darkness at the edge of her gown.

"It's all right, Clayton," she said. She laid her hand softly on Judge Silver's arm and he felt a tingle shoot from where her fingers touched him right up the back of his neck. For a split second, he believed Ida could do anything.

She smiled at the judge and said, quietly, calmly, "Clayton, I did turn Howard into a little hawk. I know you can't believe me, but I did."

Before she could go on, Bill demanded, "Tell them. Tell all of them. Tell them what you did!"

Ida was a slight woman, but in her gown, hair blossoming around her head, cloaked in a green afghan, warm golden porchlight glowing around her, the judge thought she looked like a queen. He'd always liked Ida, now he marveled at her. The crowd became hushed to hear her spare, light voice. Still she spoke only to the judge.

"I just wanted to help him," she said, "All the boys made fun of him. I've never understood why it's wrong to help people if you can. I try to be careful. This has nothing to do with Satan, for goodness sakes. It's usually not so dramatic. I never know what a healing will look like."

"She admits it then!" Bill pointed at her, "She admits it! She's a witch!"

"It didn't last!" Howard, who had moved up front to talk to Ida, protested, "I'm okay! She's nice! Leave her alone!"

"For goodness sakes. Shut up Bill! He's fine now," said Ronnie Smith. He put his hand on Howard's shoulder, "Whatever happened – Howard is fine. Better even. I don't care whether it was some sort of hypnosis or even if she is a witch, which for the record, I can't swallow any more than the judge. What are you going to do? Burn her? Nonsense. Let's all go home. No good was ever done by a mob. Looks like this thing has resolved itself."

There was a moment of quiet. Ronnie took Howard by the arm and started to lead him away. The judge took a long, calm draw on his pipe. He wasn't sure what the fallout from this would be tomorrow, but tonight he sure needed to disperse the crowd. He still thought he might be dreaming. Maybe the madness would burn off like a phantom in the morning light. The townsfolk were beginning to realize the fun was coming to an end. The old people and ladies from the Home Circle hovered nervously – surely an outright admission of witchcraft ought to provoke some sort of response. But the rest of the assembly began to melt away.

"She's a witch! She's dangerous! You have to believe me!" Bill was calling out to the retreating backs of his fellow citizens, "I saw it! She has to be stopped!"

But the judge was telling Ida that she could bring his afghan back in the morning and that maybe it would be safer to wait until the crowd had cleared to go home. He and one of the other men would walk her back themselves, or take her to her daughter's house for the evening. The judge would call one of the deputies to keep watch on the house. Just until things settled down.

Bill wasn't willing to let bygones be bygones.

"Somebody has to do something!" he shrieked. He heaved himself up to the low porch. He pushed the judge backwards, away from Ida May. Judge Silver felt Bill's pudgy fist bounce off his chest and, in his surprise, he fell to the porch floor, losing both his glasses and his pipe.

The judge was scrambling to his feet, trying to prevent Bill from reaching Ida when her slender golden arm shot out and she said something...a word the judge couldn't comprehend. Bill stopped as if something invisible had struck him in the stomach. His mouth opened into a round 'O.' He was pushed backwards, knocked off his feet by an invisible hand. Bill became darker and smaller, the ends of his arms and legs flattening and stretching out and then coiling themselves around his body, as if a snake were eating him, but that snake was himself. His eyes became wide with fright until they shrunk suddenly into glittering beads. At the very last moment, there was a small pop and he dropped, stunned, onto the porch. The judge blinked. There was nothing there except a very small black snake, blinking and flicking its tongue.

Ida's eyes opened in horror. Her hands flew to her mouth. She knelt down and leaned over the little snake hand out, steeling herself to free him from the enchantment.

But just as she was going to close her fingers on the tiny snake, Mr. Wilkerson darted like a shadow from the folds of her gown. One paw caught the tail and his shining fangs sank into the middle of the writhing body. One shake, two shakes, three. The snake went limp. Mr. Wilkerson did not release it.

There was a gasp from the crowd and then a few seconds of stunned silence, except for Myrna's moaning, which wafted around the night like the fog.

"Oh Bill! Oh Bill! O Laws! She's killed Bill! She and that devil cat have killed my Bill!"

Before the Home Circle ladies could even start calling on the Lord for help, Ida picked up the afghan from the porch floor and wrapped it around herself. She picked up the cat, snake still dangling limp from its mouth and held him to her chest, protectively. A drop of blood fell on her clean, ivory gown.

"Oh, Mr. Wilkerson," the judge heard her say softly, "Oh naughty, naughty Mr. Wilkerson."

Then...where Ida, the cat, and the dead snake had been, there was nothing. A wisp of moonlit fog swept through on the light wind and left a few curling ghosts dissolving in the night air.

Neither Bill nor Ida was ever seen again. Ever after the townsfolk swore that high, high up on the ridge, under the ancient and twisted oak that presides over Whistlestop, where the ruins of an old town, and some say a more ancient settlement linger, there is sometimes a light and sometimes smoke curling, as if from a chimney. And sometimes they say, if you walk up the path leading to the old oak a good piece, you'll see a big cat, so black it's nearly invisible, hunting in the shadows. Some of the townsfolk say that until he died, Judge Silver sometimes walked up that path in the moonlight, though no one knows how far he followed it, as there was no one in the town brave enough to tag on behind him. The judge died at the ripe old age of eighty, but on occasion the citizens of Whistlestop say they can still smell the sweet and pungent scent of cherry pipe tobacco and hear the thin sound of whistling drifting down the ridge.

The New Car

The beginning of the end was the cheap, foam mattress pad. Iris told Henry her hip was starting to hurt her. She said they needed a new mattress. She had gone down on the square to Standard's furniture and spent the better part of an hour laying on all the mattresses. The one she picked out was expensive. More than she'd paid for her first car, she had to admit it. But that memory foam topper was like a cloud. It was perfect. She told Henry about it when he got home from work that afternoon.

And then three days later he came home, carrying that cheap piece of foam in the back seat of a red, convertible Mustang, a used car he'd picked up from Dan at The Whistlestop Used Car Emporium.

"Here she is!" Henry said. He grinned at her from the driveway and patted the car, "Finally got the price I wanted from Dan, after saving all year."

"I asked for a mattress, Henry," Iris said, "I'm getting to be an old lady with bad hips. I'm not a teenager anymore. You could have put that off until after we got the mattress you know."

"Aww...c'mon, Iris. You know I've been saving up for that car since last summer. Besides, this will make you feel young again!" Henry said, waving his hand over the car like a magic carpet salesman, "We'll go on picnics! We'll take the mountain road up to Knobb Orchard and stop at Whistle Ridge Falls!"

Unfolding the foam slab from the back seat, he said, "This will make your hip feel better, I bet. I saved enough money on the car to make a good start on the mattress."

"Well, Jack, let's hope the magic beans were worth it," Iris replied. She gave the screen door a little kick on her way in to be sure he understood her feelings. The springs extended with a drawn-out screech and the door slammed shut behind her.

Of course, the mattress pad made things worse on her hip, not better. She could have predicted that. Henry's heavy body dug a ditch right in the center of the foam. He always slept right in the very middle, leaving her with an arm or a foot dangling, unless she clung desperately to the edge of the mattress. When she fell asleep, gravity rolled her bad hip down into the hollow. She woke up covered in sweat, pressed under Henry's hip and arm. Henry insisted the mattress cover just needed to get broken in.

"It's the Grand Canyon now, Henry," she said, "Don't know how much more broken in it can get."

Henry took her out in the Mustang.

"Remember how we always wanted a convertible when we first married?" Henry said. His hand was on her knee.

"I'm not a teenager anymore, Henry," she said, "This thing rides like a log truck."

Iris thought Henry looked like an idiot with the breeze from the open top puffing out two tufts of hair above his ears. She thought she remembered seeing a monkey on TV that had two puffs of hair by its ears exactly like Henry's. Her own graying hair was nothing but knots by the end of a drive, no matter how tightly she wrapped the round little bun on the back of her skull. She couldn't remember anymore why she'd ever thought a convertible was a good idea. In fact, she couldn't remember wanting one at all. Must have been Henry all along. He always thought that whatever he wanted, she wanted. She had spoiled him that way. Maybe it was because they'd never had children.

To top it all off, the Mustang's seat hurt her hip. After their first long trip over Knobb Mountain, she'd been on the couch for two days. The first day, her hip grated like the bearings had gone out. The second day was mostly to let Henry know exactly how she felt about the car. She made Henry sleep in the bed and she took the couch. She told him she didn't want to be rolling down into that ditch in the middle of the bed every night. She made sure he knew the couch was uncomfortable too.

That should have been the end of it. Henry should have seen that the Mustang wasn't the car for them, but he said they would take the car trips slow for a while – work up to all day excursions. Maybe there were some exercises she could do to make her hip feel better. He even suggested that they put the mattress on credit. She reminded him they were saving for retirement.

Iris groaned as she lowered herself into the seat whenever Henry insisted on a drive. She got out slowly and limped to picnic tables, roadside diners, the waterfall, or back inside when they got home. It was beyond time for Henry to acknowledge that he'd been wrong and sell the car. But Henry loved that Mustang. He obviously couldn't take a hint.

"Henry," she told him one morning as she poured his coffee, "The car has to go. I'm old and I have a bad hip. I need a new mattress. I didn't know what kind of shape I would be in when we agreed you could save for that car." She set the coffee pot down with a thump on the Formica table.

Henry kept his head down, staring at his coffee cup. His lower lip was trembling a little, Iris thought. What a baby!

"This is my dream, Iris!" he said into the coffee, "This is what I've wanted since I was a boy. To have a red convertible and my girl, driving around Knobb Mountain with the wind in my hair." He swirled his sugar with his spoon.

Iris dived at the table and dabbed around his cup with a dishcloth, "Be careful, Henry! You're sloshing coffee everywhere. And Lord knows you barely have enough hair for the wind to go through."

Then she sat right down in front of him and threw the dishcloth on the table. Time to lower the boom, "It's not my dream Henry. I can't dream anymore because I can't sleep. My hip hurts all the time and that cheap foam thing is just making it worse."

Henry looked straight into her eyes and with a resolve that surprised her, he said, "That's it Iris? That's been your dream all along? To be a crabby old woman with a bad hip?"

Then he got up, walked out to the car and went to work at the insurance office without saying another word.

Iris did not speak to Henry for two weeks. At first, Henry tried explaining again. Then Henry tried apologizing. He was going to try to come up with some money, but Iris needed to understand how he felt about the car. She'd already rejected putting the mattress on credit, but maybe he could sell some extra policies. He even suggested dipping into their retirement account, but Iris shook her head no. By now, she hated the car more than she wanted the mattress.

"Please, Iris," he would say, catching at her hand as she filled his coffee cup or took his plate away, "Please understand. I've always tried to give you what you want."

It was the longest Henry had ever been able to take the silent treatment without caving. Finally, Iris was tired of it.

"Henry," she said over dinner one night, "I have heard everything you've said. The sad fact of the matter is that even if you found a way to buy me that mattress tomorrow, that car hurts my hip, and I don't think you should have a car I can't ride around in. I'll be an old woman before my time."

"You've always been an old woman," Henry said, and he got up and went to their bedroom. Iris could hear him fumbling for his keys.

The screen door slammed a few minutes later and Iris heard the Mustang start with a roar. Henry revved the engine a few times and she heard him turn out onto Knobb Mountain road. The sound of the engine cut a gash in the tranquil summer evening, but soon enough Henry and the car were swallowed up by the silence, and Iris was left listening to the crickets through the open kitchen window. She sat staring at Henry's pot roast and mashed potatoes. She flung plate and all off the back stoop into the yard for the possums.

She walked to their bedroom but couldn't bear the sight nor touch of that godawful piece of foam, nor the bed that had caused all the problems in the first place. She slept on the couch.

She didn't hear from or about Henry for the next few days. He didn't call her, and she certainly wasn't going to call him. She finally heard from some friends that he was staying at the Whistlestop Inn. She saw him once or twice when she was running errands, but she refused to speak to him.

She called his receptionist at the insurance office and told her to make sure Henry understood that wherever he was, he still had a financial obligation to his wife. She expected money to be deposited into her account until he saw sense and came home, and she expected it to cover her bills.

"In fact," Iris told her, "Tell him his wife needs a new mattress."

She was sure he'd be home. After all, he wouldn't have the money to stay in a hotel much longer.

It was about three weeks later when one of her friends called, sorry, very, very, sorry to say that Henry had moved in with his receptionist. Iris saw them blasting past her porch in the red convertible once.

She did the one thing she could think of doing. She went to church. She wanted Father Dingle to call Henry and tell him that his place was with his wife and if his convertible made that impossible, then his convertible was a tool of Satan, that much seemed clear to her. Iris might go to the Episcopalian church to please Henry, but she grew up with a Baptist Granny. It wasn't just selfishness on her part either. If Henry didn't come home, that car would probably take him to the devil with it. Granny could have told him that.

Father Dingle didn't know exactly what to say. He made this clear.

"I just don't know exactly what to say," he told Iris, "I don't have that kind of power over him. Perhaps you should talk to each other. Henry has always seemed like a loving husband. You two have been married, what, thirty years now? Have you told him how much you would like him to come home? Perhaps the two of you could come to my office and talk things through. I could call and try to set things up."

Iris raised her eyebrows and looked over her bifocals at the little man.

"Surely you have some moral authority in this town," she replied, "You should tell him to come home. I don't think there's two ways about it. Don't you think that's the right thing for him to do?"

"My dear woman," said Father Dingle, "I can't force your husband to do anything. At most I can facilitate a conversation between the two of you. And, of course, pray for him."

"Hmmmph!" said Iris, and she left, letting the old oaken door of the church office fall heavily behind her.

When she got home, she thought carefully about what Father Dingle had said. Pray for Henry. She wandered over to the old pine book case and stared idly at the books for a moment. Then she saw it. Her grandmother's Bible. When any of her children or grandchildren angered her, Granny spun that wheelchair around with one hand and made a beeline to get the Bible off the shelf. Her Grandma, Myrna Cuthbert Jenkins, had married a Baptist preacher after her first husband died. Granny said if there was one thing the

Baptists knew it was that the Bible could solve any problem a human being might have.

Granny always let the Bible answer for her. Wherever it fell open, she began to read. Unsurprisingly, Granny's Bible somehow always fell open to verses calling on God to whip sinners into shape, or at the least to punish them. No wonder the old bat had outlived so many of her children, Iris thought, they probably died to get away from her. Still. Granny had known that Bible inside and out. If anyone had a doubt about what was right or wrong or who might be sinning, Iris' grandmother could set them straight.

Iris took the Bible with her to the couch, letting it fall open on her lap. The cracked leather sides fell open and whispery pages stood for a minute, fluttered, as if deciding, then settled into place.

Iris took her finger and pointed into the book, just as Granny had done from her wheelchair.

Iris read aloud, "But the wicked shall perish, and the enemies of the Lord shall be as the fat of lambs; they shall consume; into smoke shall they consume away."

That made Iris feel a good bit better. She read it again. And one more time.

"Good enough for them," Iris said. She curled up in her clothes on the couch and went to sleep. Iris woke to the jangling of the telephone. One of her friends was calling to tell her that she was sorry, very, very, sorry to have to tell Iris that Henry and his receptionist had gone off Knobb Mountain Road, right there in that bad curve going down the south side. A motorist passing by had seen smoke and when he stopped to investigate...well...her friend didn't want to go into the details. The scene had been awful. Did Iris need anything?

Iris got out Granny's Bible. She stared at it for a few minutes. The ribbon bookmark was still folded between the soft old pages at Psalm 37. She slid the book back on the shelf.

She dressed in her nightgown and got into the old oak bed for the first time since she'd argued with Henry. She put her hand out and felt the hollow place in the cheap foam mattress cover. That godawful thing was the last gift Henry had given her. Gravity pulled her toward the center. She rolled right into the hollow. Her bad hip settled into it. She breathed a sigh of relief. Without Henry there, the foam cradled her hip. The pain almost immediately lifted.

"Thank you, Jesus," she whispered, "Thank you, Henry."

A Small Haunting

My hometown had a ghost, as every small town should. Sometime in the late eighteen-hundreds, the seven-year-old daughter of a wealthy family crossed the porous border from girlhood into ghost-hood when she was thrown from her grandfather's buggy and into the path of an oncoming train. Her bereaved family erected a white marble mausoleum, a tiny, gothic Taj Mahal, behind their church. The small spired building sucked sunlight into its thick mottled shell, appearing ghostly even at noon, but glowed like polished metal in the moonlight. It formed the architecture of many of my darkest dreams. By the time I was a girl, the tomb had been there at least a hundred years.

The elaborately carved arch of pure white marble bore a curious crimson stain. Townsfolk took this to be the sign of an unrestful spirit. Other members of her family soon began to join her, an infant brother who lived only hours, her father, who died of blood poisoning after slipping on ice. When her mother was struck by an automobile, she was reunited with her little family as well. As each family member moved in, the red stain deepened. This embellishment of the family tomb was the extent of mischief our ghosts were willing to make. The story was delightfully creepy, but not too terrible for a small and fragile child like myself, a perfect haunting for a proper small town. An air of quiet sadness emanated from the little garden with the marble sepulcher at its center, a ghostly reminder of how easy it is to cross from here to there.

That's as close to a ghost as I've ever come. Until Whistlestop. One day, not too long after I inherited Aunt Nancy's house, I was sitting under the massive black oak tree in the park, down by the river, watching squirrels bustle and fuss, enjoying a moment alone. Twilight was falling as a light breeze moved the heavy air, drying the sweat under my pony tail when the air suddenly became still. I felt the hair on the back of my neck stand up, prickling like a cushion full of pins. From behind me, I heard a clicking sound, then a crackling buzz, like an old-fashioned television or radio switching on. I swung around. There was a small sandy-haired boy in a blue-checked shirt and shorts standing there, waving, a big grin on his face. His lips moved, but I couldn't make out what he was saying. Was I going deaf? I stared at him for a few seconds. Something else was wrong.

Then, suddenly, I knew. I could see the broad trunk of the oak tree right through him. I jumped. This seemed to amuse the boy. He laughed, pointed and then...switched off. He was entirely gone.

I jumped off the bench. My entire body tingled as though I was standing in the ion stream of a lightning bolt. The vanishing boy affected me in much the way that lightning would have. I ran.

I ran straight out of the park and all the way back into town, my body protesting that it was not up for such shenanigans, but I couldn't stop. I reached Joe's Diner on the Square, the only place downtown that was still open. When I got through the door, I didn't have a prayer of speaking. I just stood there panting, leaning against the nearest wall. Mary Jo Baker, namesake of her Grandpa Joe, the diner's founder, came out from behind the counter, fussing and clucking, and led me to a booth.

"Bless your heart, you look like you've seen a ghost," she said, sliding me onto a cracked vinyl seat, "I'll get you a sweet tea."

Lawrence, the proprietor of Barton and Smith's Grocery, and Angel, from the Laughing Pink Elephant antique store, were sitting at the counter. They smelled a little gossip and they both slid into the bench across the table from me.

"What's wrong?" Larry asked, "You're all out of breath. You ought not to take up jogging in shoes like that." He looked under the table at my sandals, "You'll twist your ankle."

I waved him off frowning, until I'd had a restorative sip of Mary Jo's sweet tea. It was so sweet it set my teeth on edge, but it jolted me back to life. After I'd sucked a little down, I told them what I'd seen.

Mary Jo stood with her hands in her apron pocket, listening too. She shook her head, "It was Benny," she said, then, "Your usual? You'll want to eat after a scare like that."

She didn't wait for an answer, but called to her husband Darrell in the kitchen, "Cheeseburger all the way, slaw and onion! Add an order of rings."

"Who is Benny?" I asked. Mary Jo poked her pencil through the air in Larry's direction.

"Let him tell you," Mary Jo said, "And Angel. My word, but it's been a while since anyone has seen Benny." She walked back toward the kitchen shaking her head.

"Can I have a strawberry shake, Mary Jo?" Larry called at her retreating back, "I may require further sustenance to tell this story."

"Laws, you don't need another shake, son," said Angel, pointing at his belly, "Look at that gut."

"Go home and pester Harold," Larry replied, "I'm too old to be worried about the shape of my gut."

"Guys," I said, rapping the table with my fork, "Can you cut that out and tell me if I've just seen a ghost?"

"Well," said Larry, "In a manner of speaking, I guess you have."

He turned to Angel, "What's it been? Seven years since anyone has seen Benny? Was it that year Henry McCall drove himself and his mistress off the side of Knobb Mountain?"

"Oh now, his mother saw him six years ago, right before she died. Don't you remember?" Angel said.

"She was about out of her head by then," said Larry, "Who knows."

"She said his name and darted right out into the street and got hit by a car," responded Angel with a snort, "That's good enough for me."

"Wasn't it Norton's dump truck?" Larry asked.

"Oh, now. It was, wasn't it?" Angel said, "Now were the Norton's..."

I interrupted before we were derailed by the entire history of Whistlestop, "Can someone please tell me what is going on? Who is Benny?"

"Well," Larry started, "This was years and years ago. I was a boy myself."

"So back in the stone ages?" Angel snorted at him.

"Exactly," Larry agreed, "Now if you can quit interrupting, I'll tell this story."

Benny Lewis was a fifth grader at Whistlestop Elementary when he disappeared. Benny was, in his fifth-grade teacher's words, a "pistol." (Mrs. Carmichael did not live more than five years after Benny's disappearance. Some people thought that Benny had cursed her. Then again, some people thought she deserved whatever she got. Mrs. Carmichael herself never made any après mort appearances to clear things up. As a fifth-grade teacher, she was probably just grateful for the rest.)

Benny was a kid who liked attention, any kind of attention. He liked to play baseball. If he hit the ball, he made a sweeping bow before running the bases, much to the chagrin of his teammates. If he struck out, he made a great show of throwing the bat and swinging his fist in the air. If there was a race at recess, he did a victory dance if he won. If he could tell he wasn't going to win, he would fall to the ground and cry out in anguish. More often than not, this ended the race, but he still got the attention. He liked to answer questions in class. He made this clear by waving his arms wildly, making whooping noises. If he didn't know an answer, he made one up. If there was a need for a volunteer for anything, he volunteered loudly. He brought lizards to class in his pockets and "accidentally" lost them, then made a big show of crawling around under tables looking for them. He liked to participate in the science fair every year. He made sure to bring something that belched smoke or made loud noises.

Benny's class never had a show-and-tell that didn't end with Mrs. Carmichael putting her hand on Benny's shoulder and firmly leading him back to his desk before he had finished, otherwise none of the other pupils would have had a chance. He developed a loud, horse-like laugh which he deployed whenever another student told a joke, then he would laugh until everyone begged him to stop. Mrs. Carmichael once told him to put a paper bag over his head when he did this. She said it was to prevent hyperventilation, although she might have had ulterior motives.

Poor Mrs. Carmichael. As one might suspect, the day came when she'd had enough. Benny begged loudly, wind-milling his arms, to be the one to take the roll call sheet and lunch money to the office. Mrs. Carmichael gave in and sent in him even though it was Mary Anne Jones' turn. Mary Anne sniffled loudly as Benny left.

As soon as he was gone, Mrs. Carmichael, with an air of steely resolve, walked over to Mary Anne and put her hand on the girl's shoulder.

"It's alright, Mary Anne," she said, "It's time we do something about Benny."

Every head snapped up and looked at Mrs. Carmichael. Mrs. Carmichael looked very serious. She was a tall, imposing woman with short curly permed hair that put one in mind of a brillo pad. At that moment, her lips went straight across her square face in a firm thin line. She put on her rectangular glasses and fixed her steel gray eyes on the children.

"Who's with me?" she asked. The students looked at each other. They'd never heard any teacher talk about another student that way. This was going to be an interesting day. It was about time Benny learned he wasn't the center of the universe. Mary Anne's hand went up first and then every other student followed.

Mrs. Carmichael took a Kleenex from the rubber band she kept up the polyester sleeve of her rectangular pantsuit and handed it to Mary Anne.

"Here you are, dear," she said, "Now dry those eyes. We are going to teach that young man a lesson."

Mary Anne sniffed into the Kleenex and listened with interest.

"When Benny comes back," Mrs. Carmichael said, "I don't want you to pay him the slightest bit of attention. None at all!"

The class stared at her. Mary Anne quit sniffling.

"What if he asks me a question?" asked Daniel, thoughtfully scrunching his freckled nose.

"Not if he asks you a question," said Mrs. Carmichael, "Not if he says something funny, or starts laughing that dreadful laugh of his, not if he waves his arms around in the air. Not if...anything!"

"What if he pokes me?" asked Betsey, a neat little girl with brown braids and a gingham jumper. Benny had poked her and pulled her braids on numerous occasions.

"Children, we are going to act as if Benny simply does not exist," said Mrs. Carmichael. She could tell they were somewhat confused, "As if we cannot see him or hear him. As if nothing he says or does can affect us. Even if it's very irritating. We will not look at him. We will not respond to him. We will not stop reading or doing math. No matter what he does. As far as we are concerned Benny is a ghost. We can see right through him."

"Why?" asked Martha.

"Because," said Mrs. Carmichael, her voice trembling with feeling, "He must learn that he is not the only student who deserves attention. And children?"

"Yes, Mrs. Carmichael?" responded the class.

"Anyone who does not follow these rules will be sent into the hall. We are doing this for Benny's good as well as our own. Do I make myself clear?"

"Yes, Mrs. Carmichael," the class responded in unison.

Sure enough, when Benny returned the class was as quiet as a mouse's funeral. No one spoke to him. Mrs. Carmichael didn't so much as glance up from her desk when he bounded in, slamming the door. He must have expected his usual greeting. Benny take your seat!

He stood for a moment, uncertain. Finally, he said, "I'm back! Back from the office!"

No one said anything. The other children were bent over their books. Mrs. Carmichael looked past him and out the window.

Benny walked slowly to his seat. On his way, he "accidentally" bumped Mary Anne's desk with his hip and her reading book slid sideways. She caught it without a murmur and went on reading. He sat in his desk for a few minutes, trying to catch the eye of any of his fellow students. He moved his feet loudly under his desk. He surely expected Mrs. Carmichael's usual response. Benny quit fidgeting! The response did not come.

He moved his hand over his desk. His reading book fell loudly to the floor. Swoosh! Bang!

"Sorry!" he said loudly. The children kept reading. Mrs. Carmichael got up and opened a window. The wall clock tick-tocked loudly.

Benny reached forward. Jenny, who sat in front of him, had springy golden curls. He took one by the end and sproinged it. She did not flinch. She kept reading. He kicked her chair just a little bit. He surely expected the usual response. Mrs. Carmichael! Benny is kicking my chair! Nothing.

Benny raised his hand. Mrs. Carmichael fished some more Kleenex out of her purse and tucked it into the rubber band on her arm. She rubbed some lotion on her hands, took out her grade book and set it on her desk.

"Mrs. Carmichael! I don't know what page we're on!" he waved his hand more frantically, "Mrs. Carmichael! What page are we on?"

The teacher began transferring grades from a stack of papers on her desk into the big green grade book. Benny turned to Daniel.

"Hey!" he whispered, but loudly enough so that Mrs. Carmichael could hear him, "What page are we on?"

Daniel did not respond. Benny shook Daniel's desk, but Daniel quietly turned the page of his reading book.

Benny sat for a few minutes in his chair. Then he dropped his reading book on the floor with a thud! He stood on the seat of his chair.

"Look at me!" he demanded.

Nothing. Absolutely nothing.

His head pivoted. He scanned the entire room for signs of recognition. Not one student seemed to notice that he was standing on his chair. They seemed glued to their reading books.

Benny climbed off his chair. He began stalking around the room. Stomp! Slap! He stopped at each desk and hit it with his hand.

By the time he reached the desks by the window, he was stopping in front of each student to holler, "Hey! It's me! Benny! What page are we on?"

He rapped the heads of all the boys on the last row, the girls had their hair pulled.

When he reached Martha's desk, the last one, he tried to tear her reading book from her hands, "WHAT PAGE ARE WE ON!" he yelled.

The girl clung tightly to the book without looking at Benny. Mrs. Carmichael's lips stretched into a thin, tight smile.

Benny's face was red. He stomped to the front of the classroom, hitting some of the desks on his way. STOMP! SLAP! STOMP!

He faced the class. "Look at me!" he insisted, "LOOK AT ME!"

But no one looked. He turned to Mrs. Carmichael's desk. He stood for a few long seconds contemplating his next move. His face was red, and his eyes were darting around the room.

"Hey!" he said to Mrs. Carmichael. There was no response.

He batted her potted red geranium with his open palm. The plant flew across the room and hit the wall in a shower of pottery shards and dirt. Nothing.

He stood in front of the class and sang Row, Row, Row Your Boat and Mary Had a Little Lamb as loudly as he could. The children still sat reading. The clock tick-tocked loudly. Benny could not penetrate the silence.

Mrs. Carmichael coughed gently into her Kleenex. She checked her watch to see if reading time was over.

"Keep reading quietly for ten more minutes, children," she said, "Then we will open our science books."

"Yes, Mrs. Carmichael," the children said in unison.

Benny stood in front of them. His mouth hung open for a minute. He closed it and wrapped his arms around his chest. For a moment, his bottom lip quivered. But then he pulled himself together and clenched his fists. He ran to the reading rug and whirled in circles like a dervish shouting and singing. He picked the book that Mrs. Carmichael had been reading earlier and threw it. Thunk! It bounced off of Mary Anne's desk, but she went on reading.

The intercom crackled to life. "Everything okay, Mrs. Carmichael?" asked the disembodied voice of Principal Hodges, "Disturbances have been reported down your way."

Mrs. Carmichael allowed her eyes to drift around the room. Her gaze slid past Benny.

"No, we're fine here," she said, cheerfully, "Must be Mr. Carter's class next door."

Benny stopped in his tracks. He sat down on the reading rug, thinking. He hugged his knees for a few minutes, then he finally stood up.

"That's it!" he said, "I'm invisible! I can do whatever I want!"

He walked to the treasure box where Mrs. Carmichael kept rewards for well-behaved children. Seldom had Benny been allowed to choose a prize. He reached his hand in and scooped out treasures. Marbles, green army men and cheap bottles of soap bubbles fell to the ground. He stuffed his pockets. He ran to his back pack and pulled out bubble gum. He stuffed his mouth with it and began blowing giant pink bubbles and popping them. He opened all the windows and spat the giant wad of gum onto the sidewalk.

"Hooray!" he said, "I can do what I want!"

He went into the cloak room. After some rustling around there was a loud clanging and banging. He came out with a banana and a ham sandwich and sat down on the rug, chewing loudly.

Still no one had acknowledged him. After he ate, he sat very, very still. He put his head in his hands.

"I don't like being invisible anymore," he said, "I'm lonely. Lonely, lonely, lonely. Can anybody hear me?" A single tear slid down his cheek.

Mrs. Carmichael was beginning to feel that she had made her point. To be on the safe side, she decided to wait five minutes to allow Benny to process his feelings. Those five minutes were the only ones she would ever admit regretting.

Another tear fell as Benny sat on the reading rug, then another. "I guess no one likes me," he said. With the unabashed heartlessness that comes so naturally to children, the other students still sat reading.

The teacher finally arose. She would tell the class that it was time to let Benny in on their secret. She would explain to Benny that if he could now be a nice quiet little boy, they might all acknowledge his presence.

"Now class," she began. The children looked up, ready to have the joke over with so they could rib Benny, but before she could finish, Benny stood up.

He stamped his foot and shrieked, "Fine! I hate you all and I will be invisible. Forever!"

And with that Benny disappeared.

Some of the children were looking at Mrs. Carmichael when the vanishing occurred, but a good number were looking right at Benny, as was their teacher. Their stories were all exactly alike. One minute, Benny was there. The next minute, Benny was gone. A few of them said he flickered once or twice like a bad television signal.

After Principal Hodges pieced together the baffling story from the accounts of twenty hysterical students and one panic-stricken teacher, he called the Sheriff. Of course, Benny's parents had to be notified. They all searched the room and the school building and the surrounding woods thoroughly and came up with exactly nothing.

Mrs. Carmichael was put on leave for losing, if not murdering one of her pupils. There was no hard evidence that she had done any such thing and she had twenty-one witnesses who agreed with the story as she told it. The children and Mrs. Carmichael stuck to their story like glue.

Benny's mother, Christine Lewis, wanted Mrs. Carmichael arrested, for egregious incompetence if nothing else. From this she would not budge no matter how many times the Sheriff told her there was no such law. John Lewis, Benny's father, was inclined to think that Benny had somehow disappeared as a joke, maybe run away, but he couldn't understand how no trace of him had ever found inside or outside of the classroom.

The Lewises organized search parties for their only child. They took out newspaper ads and put up posters and flyers. All of it was useless. The whole town turned out to support them, searching the woods and dredging the lake. The company where Mr. Lewis was an engineer put up ten thousand dollars in reward money. After three weeks, it began to look as if Benny had simply vanished. The town kept a strict eye on its children but still...life had to go on. The citizens began to go quietly about their business again.

At just about that time, the situation became slightly more complicated. Mrs. Lewis was getting dinner for her husband. She tearfully set an extra place for Benny, something she had insisted on doing every night since his disappearance. When she came to the table with the bread plate she was shocked to see Benny sitting in his chair, grinning at her. At first, his mother said, he looked perfectly normal.

"Benny!" she said, "Where have you been, pumpkin?"

Then she dropped the bread plate right on the floor and screamed. She could see right through her son to the chair behind him. Benny's father came running into the kitchen just in time to see his son fade into nothing.

As he blinked out of existence they both heard his voice, distant and crackling, say, "Ha! Ha! I'm invisible!"

After that, Benny was spotted in the park, on the playground, in the bell tower at the church, in a boat on the lake. Once someone claimed to have seen him standing in the middle of the train tracks laughing as a train barreled towards him. Of course, a lot of people were probably just caught up in the excitement of the whole thing. It was hard for a little while to distinguish who had actually seen Benny and who just really, really wanted to see him. Some of the townspeople said that the sightings proved that Mrs. Carmichael had killed him because the visitations must be manifestations of his ghost.

Mr. Lewis, an engineer and one of the few open atheists in town, could accept no such thing. He believed that his son had slipped off the space/time continuum and into some wormhole in the universe. Mrs. Lewis came to believe the same thing, not because she was rationally convinced of it, but because it gave her hope. Perhaps science could return her lost boy to her someday.

The visitations occurred with less frequency over the years. Benny's parents could often be seen in the places where someone claimed to have seen Benny, wandering around and calling for him. His father studied any kind of science or pseudo-science, from the most respected physicists to the weirdest old cranks as long as it had to do with strange disappearances, alternate realities, or wormholes. He was looking for any cracks in the universe that a young boy could fall through. By the time he died, Mr. Lewis had become quite a weird old crank himself. Mrs. Lewis still held onto the faint hope that someday, somehow, Benny would find a way to return to her, even though on every occasion that he manifested, he seemed positively gleeful about being invisible. Ultimately, Benny had the last laugh. His mother's last act was to call out his name and step in front of a dump truck on Main Street.

"And that," finished Larry, "Is the story as I know it."

"So," I said with a sigh, "One more thing that's weird about Whistlestop. It can't even have a proper ghost."

"Hmmppph!" said Angel, and she tossed her thick gray hair over her shoulder, "Do they have a rule book for ghosts where you come from, Missy? I guess he's as good a ghost as haunted any other town," she stood up and sighed, "Anyway, I'd best be going. Harold's waiting at home for me."

After the diner door closed behind her, I turned to Larry, "Sorry," I said, "I think I've offended Angel."

"I wouldn't worry too much about it," Larry said, "I don't think Benny's a ghost at all. Not in the usual way. Mr. Lewis was right. I think there's some scientific explanation for the whole thing. I've never figured out why church people would rather believe in ghosts than wormholes."

He fished around in the bottom of his shake glass for his cherry.

"What do you think happened?" I asked.

"I don't know," he responded, "I can tell you this. I was in that classroom when Benny disappeared. I was one of the kids staring right at him when he vanished. Saw him flicker like a flame, kinda staticky. And then there's this," he leaned over the table, "A couple of weeks after he disappeared, I was down behind Whistlestop Elementary all by myself, kicking a ball around. Lord, my mother would have whipped my butt if she found out. For all we knew someone had killed him. Parents were going nuts the first few weeks. I kicked the ball and retrieved it a few times and the last time, just as I kicked it, I saw Benny. He laughed and grabbed the ball with his see-through hands. Then he and the ball disappeared."

Larry sat back in his seat, "Does that sound like a ghost to you?"

"I guess not," I said.

"The other thing is," Larry said, "Whenever someone sees Benny, at least most of the most believable sightings, there's always a bad electrical storm the same day. There was a storm the day he disappeared, the day his mother saw him, the day I saw him.

"Hear that?" Larry pointed out the window.

A loud crack of thunder pealed out over Knobb Mountain. A streak of lightning lit up a cloud.

"There's your storm," he said, "The other thing is that sometimes after someone sees him, something goes missing. Sometimes it's a kid's bike, sometimes a pet. There have even been a few people go missing from this town. Whether it has to do with Benny, or some portal to another dimension, I don't know."

Larry slid out of the booth. As he reached the door he turned and said, "You better get home. Looks like it's going to be a bad one."

The thunder rolled off the mountain, "Too late. I think I'll wait for Mary Jo to close up and go home with her," I responded, "Maybe the storm will pass by then."

"Maybe so," Larry said, with a shrug, "Maybe so."

He opened the door, then paused and turned, "But don't get your hopes up. There's always another storm coming in Whistlestop."

A Cautionary Tale

The very best part of spending every summer in Whistlestop was my Aunt Nancy, partly because she let me read whatever I wanted without question, partly because she never enforced any bedtime whatsoever, so I was never forced to hide under a blanket with a flashlight. Of course, she also loved books and stories. When I was very little, she read to me or made up her own stories every night I stayed with her. Although, I loved and still love all the books she read to me, from The Hobbit to Rose in Bloom, the best nights were when she told me her own loopy bedtime stories.

I can still remember her, sitting in the chair next to my bed, one slim leg folded under her, her black cat, Hoppy, in her lap, twirling a piece of hair that had escaped from her loose bun, dark blue eyes staring past me out the window into the summer night and telling the story that she saw there. As I got sleepy, I always had a vague fancy that the stories grew on the old crabapple tree just outside my bedroom window, that she somehow saw them quivering there on the summer breeze.

I never understood why my vivid, tall, beautiful aunt stayed in the little town. Although Aunt Nancy was older than my father, she seemed younger. She dressed in colorful stylish clothes that made her stand out like a sore thumb in the little town, and she had opinions, few of them positive, few of them popular, that she expressed at town meetings and in editorials. The church ladies were wary of her, and she had only a few good friends there in town. In fact, she traveled extensively. I always suspected that was because there's only so much Whistlestop a rational human can take, but she always went back to her little farmhouse, the one she'd shared with her husband James until he died at fifty-three.

When I asked her about it, she said, "This town needs me. Goodness, what dreadful places small towns would be if they could decide who should stay and who should go. It's good for them to have people who make them think outside the box. I wouldn't feel right leaving them to their own devices. It would be cruel."

After that, she told me bedtime stories about a small town she called Possum Cove, a town that bore an uncanny resemblance to Whistlestop. Many things happened in Possum Cove that had a rhyming similarity to our little mountain town. We both added details and characters as I grew up. The following story is one of her best.

Once there was a beautiful little town on a mountain called Possum Cove. The townsfolk seemed vaguely embarrassed by the name. When asked about the history of the name they swore that the Cherokee had called it that for millennia, but, of course, there were no Cherokee left to ask. The townspeople's forefathers and foremothers had driven them away long before.

Possum Cove, other than the name, might have been the perfect picture of a small town. The town square boasted a large white Victorian bandstand where crowds often gathered late into warm evenings to hear barbershop quartets or the high school band. There was a beautiful park with picnic tables centered on an ancient, spreading oak, and twisting, maple-lined roads that slid smoothly past rows of beautiful homes, from neat brick cottages to frilly Victorians. When the snows came, and the rosy cheeked children flocked to the hillsides with their sleds and brightly-colored hats and mittens, the town looked like it had been plucked from a Christmas card and brought to life.

There was a downside to life in Possum Cove though. In the winter, the snow and ice on the mountains surrounding the tiny town blocked the roads, so inhabitants who chose not to leave before the snows began were stuck there for most of the winter. In the summer, mudslides on the mountain had a similar effect. The citizens had to carefully consider their needs for the year and order far more food and other goods than they really needed just to be on the safe side. This made them a very practical people. The very rare newcomer to Possum Cove noticed a certain lack of imagination and a great deal of concern with buying provisions, having them delivered, and storing them. Anyone might be forgiven for thinking the whole town was a sort of open-air asylum for hoarders. For instance, old Dr. Benjamin H. Johnston had suffered brain damage when he was hit by a pallet of canned beans that he had unwisely stacked atop several pallets of paper towels and toilet paper. The whole mountain of canned goods and paper goods had finally become weak, and one winter morning when he went into his basement to look for a can of tuna for his cats, the paper towels gave way and the tower of canned beans toppled over on his head. After that, he became very confused and tried numerous times to feed the beans to the cats. Eventually, they ate him. (However, that's another of Aunt Nancy's stories entirely.)

No...this particular tale revolves around someone entirely different, a man named Geoffrey. Geoffrey was an attorney in the town—actually, the attorney. As you might expect, he had quite a roaring business. After all, though the town was small and of a bucolic and peaceful appearance, these people were completely stuck with each other for at least nine months of the year. As such, they got into the most terrible legal disputes, partly out of boredom. Of course, this was good for Geoffrey. He was quite the richest man in town. His stack of groceries and other goods was three times higher than anyone else's. One late winter morning he was working very hard to make it four times higher; in the interest of this goal, he was preparing a spreadsheet to predict which of his neighbors' petty disputes might be fanned into legal flame when, according to his friends and neighbors (well, mostly neighbors, as the town's only attorney he didn't have many friends), his brain must have broken. He was right in the middle of thinking of ways he could encourage the Smiths to enter a long and acrimonious divorce when he suddenly lost his taste for the law. He got up from his office chair and never returned.

At first, this brain brokenness revealed itself in mere agitation. He could barely sit for a few moments before he had to stand. He could stand for only a few seconds before he needed to move into another room. He could barely stay in that room for a few seconds before he needed to move to another room. He could barely stay focused long enough to remember to go to the toilet. (And sometimes he couldn't).

His neighbors noticed him muttering as he wandered aimlessly around the town, sitting on benches, then standing, then running, occasionally asking directions to the nearest public toilets. As his troubles grew deeper and more apparent, the townsfolk often pointed out the public restrooms before he could even ask. He was saying things like, "Four is not as much as five. Is five enough? Could it be more? What is the last number? Why infinity? Then I can never have enough."

The concept of infinity was a constant in his muttering, a taunting goal, an abstraction Geoffrey seemed to think existed only to make him feel small and inadequate. Sometimes he would ask directions to infinity, which brought him nothing but troubled looks and explanations that infinity wasn't a place. One day he made it a point to ask every person in town to tell him the last number of all. The one that made infinity a moot point. That was the number he was after. He did not like feeling small. Feeling small made him feel afraid. Feeling afraid made him feel angry, although he did not know why.

When asked for the last number, most of the townspeople merely answered contemptuously that there was no such thing. Only May Anna Clark, a sturdy three year old in pink overalls, made the attempt.

"Eighty-ten," she said decisively, as that was the only number that came to mind, and it seemed large enough to be impressive.

After this he wandered around town muttering "Eighty-ten" to himself for some time, shaking his head.

Finally, he came to a conclusion. "It can't be stopped," he would say. "Infinity can't be stopped."

After that his question to the townsfolk was, "Aren't you afraid of infinity? It can't be stopped, and no one can reach the end of it."

He received various answers. May Anna Clark simply stared at him and continued to lick her red swirled sucker as it dripped down her chin; she rightly guessed that a number wouldn't answer this question.

Dr. Benjamin Johnston (while he was still extant), replied, "No. I'm afraid of my cats."

Ellen Smith, who was very much in love with her husband and who did not want an acrimonious divorce, said, "No. But I'm afraid that Charles might leave me someday."

Martin Elliot said, "I'm afraid we're never going to have another attorney, and I would really like to sue the Marcotts because their dog keeps pooping in my yard."

All in all, none of the answers was satisfactory. But he kept doggedly going from house to house, to the park, and to the market to ask everyone he could find. He walked through the white picket fence with the red roses at the Andersons' historic home with the broad porches and frightened the maid with the question. He found the Carpenters behind their red brick cottage on the patio, enjoying drinks, but they were about halfway to infinity themselves and found his question immoderately hilarious. He accosted Mr. Jones at the old fashioned two pump gas station that still had an attendant, but Mr. Jones just laughed and told him he was crazy. He was even less successful questioning two young couples entwined under the giant oak at the park, and when he interrupted a pick-up baseball game, the teenagers actually threw the ball at his head.

He didn't get an answer that helped him at all until he came to question the last person in town. It was the English instructor, Ms. Schmidt. She was an outsider, young and opinionated, who had recently graduated the university and she was perhaps used to looking at questions more academically than the rest of the people in town, especially since she had gone through two years of graduate school and was now finishing her thesis. Emily Schmidt had begun to suspect that living in this town probably would make a person crazy eventually, and she really couldn't blame Geoffrey for finally going round the twist. In fact, in a way it seemed the most logical response to this place. She liked him better as a lunatic, in fact; except for the occasional strong smell of urine, she might have begun to find him quite attractive with his strange questions and deep brown eyes. As for Geoffrey, he was probably predisposed to listen to Ms. Emily Schmidt. He had been quite attracted to her pale freckled skin and the serious tortoiseshell glasses that framed her bright green eyes. He only kept himself from asking her out by reminding himself how expensive a divorce could be. He had had a nightmare that involved her coming with a dump truck to take half his stack of stored goods.

What Emily Schmidt said was this, "Infinity is a silly thing to be worried about, Geoffrey. It's too big and you can't get your mind wrapped around it. You can't do anything about it. You need to find something more concrete to worry about."

And suddenly he realized...she was right. Infinity was far too large and heavy. Infinity was an elephant. His worry was ant-sized in comparison. He suddenly pictured himself as an ant with a tiny spear desperately poking at the toe of the behemoth. No matter how crushingly heavy the weight of his fear and anger felt to him, it would never affect infinity. No, Emily was right. It would never do. He needed something to embody his fears. Something to blame. Something concrete and REAL and relatively small, a skin to wrap around his dreadful angst and anger and fear of inadequacy.

So, from that day forth, Geoffrey was afraid of...giraffes. No one knew exactly how it happened. As a matter of fact, some of the townsfolk who had spent their whole lives there weren't too sure what a giraffe was until Geoffrey started going on about them. Of course, they had seen them in school books and library books, but giraffes had never really registered in their minds. They were a practical and incurious people and honestly didn't have any need to know about such exotic and unlikely creatures. Almost all of the citizens of Possum Cove were of pretty much the same mind. Teach the practical. Teach what you know will be encountered. Giraffes were an unnecessary bit of fluff and fantasy. No real point to them.

When Geoffrey transferred his fear from Infinity to Giraffes, it was spring in the town. The Sun was beginning to peek out from behind the mountains earlier and earlier. The air had quit slapping the towns folk in the cheeks every time they walked out the door and sometimes caressed and cajoled them instead, like a psychotic and changeable lover. Every moment of warmth and light needed to be used, gardens dug, possessions aired out, streets and roofs mended. So, when Geoffrey began his speeches in the public square, there were almost always people available to hear him.

He spoke about the great and terrible size of the giraffe. He preached about the aggression of the male giraffe during mating season. He had large poster displays of giraffes. On some of them he had obviously painted devil horns and mustaches. He had pictures, which he had obviously drawn himself, depicting giraffes committing bank robberies and picking pockets. He once gave a long speech on the terrible music taste of giraffes – he referenced heavy metal and had three very under-ripe tomatoes thrown at him by several of the baseball players he had previously inconvenienced. He returned the next day in spite of his black eye. This time he had some very graphic although badly drawn pictures of a gang of giraffes murdering a chimpanzee. His pleas were very heartfelt, though obviously insane. Emily felt more and more sorry for him every day. And then a funny thing happened.

A few people in the town began to display a slight prejudice against giraffes. The town librarian was taken to task for displaying a children's book that pictured a giraffe for the letter "G." Actually, this always rather annoyed Emily too, but only because she felt it was too confusing to represent the soft "g" sound instead of the hard "g" of goat. Emily had been sitting at the library preparing for an upcoming class because she loved the smell of the old building and the way the light poured in through the tall leaded windows onto her book, when a frazzled looking woman came in dragging her four-year-old child by the hand. The child was gripping a book with The Animal ABCs printed in a bright cartoony font on the front cover.

"But I like it, Mommy," the child was saying.

The woman looked a little disconcerted and handed the book to the librarian. She looked around to see if anyone was listening and then said, in an almost apologetic tone, "You see, it has a giraffe in it. So, if we could just return it. Please."

The librarian looked confused. "A giraffe? But I don't exactly see the problem?"

The mother looked around again and bit her lip. "Well, of course, I read this book when I was young, but that man keeps talking about them doesn't he? And he," she paused to jerk her head at the child, "Well, he had a nightmare about a giraffe just the other day, didn't he?"

"I wouldn't know," said the librarian, perhaps feeling somewhat accused. "I mean, you can bring back a book and get another one any time. You don't actually have to ask, you know."

"Well," said the harassed mother, "I'm telling you this because...well, because, you know he might not be the only one. I'm just not sure that children should be reading this book. You know.... maybe not right now." She clung fiercely and protectively to the little boy's hand, though he was squirming so that Emily wondered how his arm remained in its socket.

"I would think," said the librarian – he was looking increasingly exasperated, "that he might benefit from seeing a friendly and happy giraffe. That seems like the best cure for his nightmares."

"Oh no," said the offended mother. "I really just don't think...He's four, you know. Please just take it back."

"Doesn't he want to choose another?" asked the librarian.

"I just..." she stopped as the child nearly twisted out of her arm. "I just don't know. Maybe later." And she scurried out.

The only good thing that came out of the encounter was that Emily made friends with Eddie, the town librarian. Because from that day on, things slowly started to deteriorate, and they needed each other.

Several mothers complained. They knew, of course they knew, that giraffes weren't so bad, it was just that right now the kids were afraid of them. Some of their little ones had been having nightmares. They knew that giraffes didn't commit bank robberies or murder chimpanzees. Of course not. But the aggression was real. A group of worried mothers sent away for a book on giraffes and were shocked by the aggression of the mating males. Maybe giraffes were more dangerous than they thought. Some of the mothers took it upon themselves to remove any book from the library that had any information on giraffes. Just to prevent nightmares of course. And Geoffrey was an educated man. He had a law degree, for goodness' sakes. There had to be some truth to whatever he might say.

And some of the townsfolk, particularly those who had been the most prone to suing their neighbors after a long boring winter, began to agitate against giraffes as well. It seemed to be a sort of outlet for some of the simmering unrest created by the feeling of entrapment, the same sort of outlet that suing each other had been. Geoffrey was really no longer capable of aiding them with their former pastime. The idea that giraffes were evil caught some sort of swirling current in this town of oddly practical people. It began to spread like a disease. The preacher at the old town church used the giraffe as a metaphor for wickedness. When confronted by Emily about this, he replied that he didn't believe all of that nonsense himself, but it was a handy tool since his parishioners did believe it. School teachers began to tell their students to behave like humans and not giraffes.

In vain, Emily and Eddie protested that giraffes were grazing animals. They were actually quite peaceful. And they were not a threat to the town at all. No giraffes lived anywhere near the town. Emily tried to teach a lesson on giraffes but was reported to the principal who told her in no uncertain terms that his job depended on the parents trust and buy-in. It was all she could do not to hit him. (She felt almost ethically compelled to punch people who used buzzwords like buy-in under the best of circumstances.) He noted that, of course, he didn't believe any of that nonsense at all, but who was he to question the parents of his students. And what was the harm? There were no giraffes here in the town.

The whole thing came to a head one day when she was jogging in the park with Eddie. One of her students came running up to them and said simply, "You've got to see this." They followed her to the town square, dread weighing so deeply on Emily that she was silent until she saw the terrible sight. Almost half the population of the town had turned out for an anti-giraffe protest. Speaker after speaker took the stage to spout terrible and egregiously false facts about giraffes. Oddly, they didn't all agree with one another, but most seemed to agree that giraffes were an awful and growing problem. One speaker claimed that they were an alien race who had come and waited a hundred thousand years, grazing, but that soon they would throw off their disguises and take over the earth. Most people disagreed with this premise, but Emily could hear them grunting things like, "Well, of course, the fact that he's crazy doesn't prove that giraffes are not disagreeable."

One man claimed that it had been proven that giraffes consumed so much vegetation including gardens and fields of crops that children who lived in countries where giraffes were found suffered and died from starvation. This was less outrageous than the previous claim and no one had proof to the contrary, so the majority of the crowd seemed to agree that it was probably true. Someone else spoke about a rumor she had heard that the government would be releasing wild giraffes into the mountains around the town. When one man was heard to question the ability of giraffes to live in the mountains, the woman told him that she had heard the government had bred certain giraffes for this special purpose.

After about an hour of this madness, Emily felt a tug on her sweater. It was Eddie. He made a brief gesture toward some of the crowd at the back of the square close to where he and Emily were standing. Three older men stood staring at them, arms crossed, legs squarely apart, frowning. Apparently, Emily and Eddie had made their status as doubters too well known. "Time to go," Eddie whispered.

Emily and Eddie made the rounds and talked to the half of the townspeople who had chosen not to attend the protest. The Carpenters were three sheets to the wind as always and they found the whole situation funny. The Smiths said quite frankly that they were afraid to say anything, and they couldn't see why they should risk angering their neighbors over something that wasn't a problem in the first place. The whole thing was a fantasy, and it wouldn't affect the town in the long run. Emily tried to note that since this particular fantasy was creating an atmosphere of fear and anger perhaps it was important, but the Smiths assured her that they figured the whole thing would blow over by fall. And so, it went. The people who did not attend the anti-giraffe protest refused to consider it a problem, or they were afraid to consider it a problem, or they simply didn't care because it didn't really affect anyone.

As a last resort, they tried talking to Geoffrey. They found him sitting alone on a park bench, smiling and singing to himself. Oddly, he seemed far less agitated by the situation than the rest of the townspeople.

Emily tried first, "Geoffrey, please tell me you know all this stuff about giraffes is not true."

Geoffrey simply smiled at her. "What is truth, Emily? The people have fears. They have anger. They need somewhere to place it. Why not a creature that lives far from here, a creature they need never deal with at all. Why not take that angst and burn it up in public anger and then send it far away from us? We will all be better for it."

Eddie recoiled. He said, "No one has ever been better for believing a lie, Geoffrey."

Geoffrey smiled peacefully, "It isn't a lie as such, you see. It's an allegory of sorts. I am calmer now because I have taken all the badness and sadness and anger out of myself and given it to a creature far, far away where I will never have to deal with it again. Don't you see what peace I have? Why can't they all have that same peace? Why will you deny them peace?"

"That's not peace!" said Emily. "Geoffrey, they are not at peace. They are angry, and they are becoming angrier at each other. You can't gain peace by believing something that's...that isn't true because it will only lead to endless arguments. They are starting to fight with each other and to split into factions. You have to tell them that you made all of that stuff up."

"No," Geoffrey said quietly. "That will never do. They will burn through the anger. They will let out their badness and the giraffes will gallop away with it, using it to fuel their own aggressions which evolution has given them as a tool for survival. We will all be better for it. Let the anger burn. It will burn away as mine did."

Eddie spoke up, "Your anger didn't burn away, buddy. Your brain did."

Geoffrey replied, "Infinity is frightening. We can't do anything about it. Infinity is real and engulfs us at every turn. It's best to be frightened of smaller things. You told me so yourself, Emily." Here he reached for Emily's hand and patted it.

"That's not what I meant, Geoffrey. It's best to be frightened of things you can confront. Things you can do something about. Like stopping this really scary lie," said Emily. And for one second, Geoffrey's eyes opened, and he seemed to see her. But it faded almost immediately, and his eyes drooped again, back into beatific complacency.

Emily started to speak up again, but Eddie tugged her arm. "It's no use, Em. He's gone." And they left. They packed their bags and Eddie's cat Gordon and left the town that night. Emily's small car was stuffed to the brim and they drove out at midnight to the soft yowls of Gordon, who was not a happy traveler.

On the way out of town, Emily noted, "Well, I guess they are just not a metaphorical people. They take things way too literally."

"No, Em," said Eddie, "They are an extremely metaphorical bunch. If they knew that, they would be okay. It's the fact they think they're being practical that's killing them."

By the next spring, the town was in shambles. There were posters of giraffes in nefarious poses pasted all around the town, but there were also posters of hippos in suggestive poses, hippos shooting guns, hippos shooting heroin, or hippos committing violent crimes. The warm wind blew pieces of torn posters and banners playfully through the streets, as if to convince the residents to lighten up already, but the mood was not light. There were weekly protests in the town square, but sometimes the protestors were protesting other protestors. The town was now split into factions because Mrs. Harriet Gunderson, who ran the town post office, had come to the conclusion that hippopotami were the real problem and were far more evil than giraffes. While reading an article about giraffes, she happened to notice that more people were killed by hippos than any of the large predators in Africa, and immediately she realized that hippos were the real killers.

People lost jobs because they believed in the evils of giraffes or because they were hippo people, or vice versa. There was a spaced-out-looking hippo painted in thick, dripping black paint on the side of Mr. Walter's pristine white Victorian house. Some graffiti artist had painted a giraffe with devil horns on the courthouse wall. There were posters and poorly painted animals all over town. There were houses with broken windows. The poor sheriff had finally given up on trying to discipline people for such actions. The town jail only held twelve people at a time.

The people who really didn't believe any of the stories tried to go quietly about their jobs without saying much of anything. This tactic met with varying levels of success. Even the Carpenters had to sober up a little to avoid saying the wrong things to the wrong people. It had been a rough winter with no ingress of supplies at all for months on end and people were starting to eye the basements and attics of their neighbors, especially those on the opposite side of the giraffe question. Only Geoffrey seemed calm, and he would occasionally pop up at a neighbor's house bearing a gift from his stash. Even the hippo people saw him as a sort of prophet, and everyone had great respect for his wide-eyed sayings and air of preternatural calm. He had now taken to wearing a sheet around his shoulders, almost as a cape, and it fluttered around his threadbare suits as he walked the town.

It seemed that things might go on this way forever. But one day there was a change in the wind.

It was a bright and balmy day and there was a strange scent hanging in the air, hot, bright, and pungent. It was an exotic smell. And from deep in the mountains, there was a sort of rumbling. At first, many people believed it was the roaring of the streams from the melting snow. This added a certain nervous tension to the atmosphere since flash floods often delayed the shipment of goods. The rumbling grew louder. Geoffrey went from door to door, quietly asking everyone to meet in the town square for an important assembly. Though his demeanor was quiet, his eyes were large and wild. It was a potent combination and most of the townspeople obliged him. The hippo people gathered to the right side of the gazebo and the giraffe people to the left. As the people gathered, Geoffrey stood in the middle of the gazebo smiling like a happy child and waving them closer. The crowd, which had been muttering and buzzing to itself, stood silent and watched him with wonder. Geoffrey began to remind them of all of the things they had believed about giraffes and all of the evils of giraffes. As the hippo people began to murmur against him, he turned to them with compassion and told them lovingly that all they believed might be true and that one thing did not necessarily cancel out the other. They might be right to hate and fear both hippos and giraffes. And then he paused, hand held sharply over his eyes, looking into the glaring sun. The rumbling became louder. Though no one noticed it but Geoffrey, a small car pulled up in the public parking lot across Main Street under a large and sturdy oak tree.

Geoffrey smiled and raised his hands to the skies. He shouted above the rumbling din, "A wise woman once told me that the only way to defeat fear is to face it. I did not believe her then, but I have been humbled. You have humbled me with your inability to find peace. Behold your fear! Face it!" Geoffrey then leapt from the gazebo and walked through the crowd toward the growing clamor. He waved at two small figures that had left the car and had climbed up the massive old oak.

"Emily! Eddie! I'm glad you could come!" he called out.

One of the figures raised a red bullhorn to its lips. The people could barely hear the voice, "Run! Run for your lives!"

This strange warning did not move the towns people. Perhaps they were confused by the thundering of hooves and the odd hot smell in the air. Perhaps they didn't know what to believe any more. At any rate, they were totally unprepared when the stampede of giraffes exploded into the square. Many of them hardly had time to think at all. One survivor remembered a great golden knot whirring and pushing in the direction of the square, brushing past the oak tree, swaying the two, small people hidden in its branches but not dislodging them. He remembered thinking that the oak tree would have been a good place to be. And then the herd was upon them, a tangle of limbs and dust, screams and the sounds of cracking bone. He remembered the smell of blood and then a thick force pushed his head into a well of blackness. That was all.

After it was over, while the survivors tended to the wounded and dying, Emily leaned over Geoffrey's battered form. He was twisted almost beyond recognition, the sheet wound around his neck. He was struggling for breath and one arm was pinned beneath him.

"You were right, Emily." He reached for her with his good hand. "They could not release their fears as I could." He coughed for a bit, spitting out blood. "They had to face them."

"Oh Geoffrey, you moron," said Emily, "You are always misinterpreting me. Giraffes only stampede if you frighten them. You should have shown them that they were peaceful grazing animals. You must confront fear with the truth."

But it was too late. Geoffrey was dead. The wind blew in a great gust over the field of death and wreckage. A small white card fluttered by in the wind. Emily picked it up and read, "Stampedes 'R' Us – Exotic Animal Rentals." She noticed May Anna standing at the side of the square, open-mouthed, staring at the carnage. She took the little girl's hand and walked to Eddie and said, "While they clean this up, let's call the auto club and then go hang out at the library until they get here."

The Bite

Mrs. Mary Edelson Brookes was a woman whose main claim to fame in the town of Whistlestop was her ability to throw stylish dinner parties; she was also known for her ability to wear exactly the right shoes with exactly the right purse without being too "matchy," the fact that her hair always looked "done," and because her hybrid tea roses almost always took a prize at the flower show. In addition, she was on three church committees and the town beautification board. Although the difficulty of these achievements was impossible to disregard, Mary was otherwise not the most fascinating person in town. In fact, if you asked her husband Bob, he would have called her stable and meant it as a compliment. Her seventeen-year old daughter, Virginia, would have called her boring and not meant it as a compliment at all. But, as the townspeople noted afterwards, you don't have to be a fascinating person to have something interesting happen to you.

The story recounted here is a strange one and it's hard to say exactly what did happen to Mary that hot and humid summer. Accounts vary. The story told by the few people closest to Mary is the one that most thoroughly explains the situation. Unfortunately, it's also the most difficult to believe. But strange things were afoot in Whistlestop in those days.

Mary lived in an imposing Georgian house of sand-colored brick with a formal portico at the front and neat clipped hedges lining the walkway. In back, were her prize roses. Of all the things that Mary loved, her hybrid tea roses were secretly at the top of the list. In her back yard, by the picket fence, she had a long bed full of them. Each rose was labeled and stood proud and alone in its spot. An emerald green lawn stretched in front of the rose bed, neat and expansive. Each rose plant was pinched back so that just a few pointed buds were left to mature into fat, fragrant blossoms. She carefully, sprayed them to keep them free of insects and diseases. When Mary was in her yard, with her perfect roses, it seemed that life itself was perfect. A certain busyness ruled Mary's life, but on rare occasions she would find herself lost in the fragrance or form of a rose.

There were two things that seriously thwarted Mary's pursuit of perfection. First, there was her neighbor Isabelle's garden. It backed up to Mary's rose garden like a stripper doing a lap dance for a man wearing an expensive watch. Isabelle's garden was almost the exact opposite of Mary's, lush, dense, and sensual, dominated by the whims of nature, not the firm hand of the gardener; Mary was constantly fighting stray tendrils of sweet peas that pushed through the fence slats, or peppermint or blackberries that simply bypassed the fence and thrust themselves up through the yard right between the knees of one of the grand hybrid teas. The tawdry scent of gardenia, lilac or tuberose often overwhelmed Mary while she tended her roses. She sometimes found herself hurriedly bending down to pluck a bit of naughty lemon balm or catmint from beneath her roses. The absolute bane of Mary's gardening existence was a giant butterfly bush that sprawled its scraggly arms across the fence and shaded out the raspberry colored Auguste Renoir in the corner. The old butterfly bush sometimes nudged off Mary's wide brimmed garden hat with a long twiggy finger. Mary wasn't much given to nonsense, but the shrub seemed almost sentient in its attempts to annoy her.

Mary's other nemesis was her daughter Virginia. Virginia's roots were constantly slipping beyond fences and into the wilds; her untamed tendrils seemed determined both to invade and escape Mary's soft, small and comfortable world. Some sort of spraying or pruning was definitely in order, but as anyone could see, Mary had never quite determined how such a thing might be accomplished. As with the butterfly bush, every effort to restrain Virginia seemed to result in even more vigorous and spiraling disorder. Virginia's dyed black hair, books of dark poetry, strange dissonant music and habit of crawling out her window at night to paint pictures of the moon were frightening to Mary and amusing to the townsfolk. As an added insult, Virginia had since childhood preferred Isabelle's garden and now that she was a teenager often went there to paint, even in the middle of the night. Once, when asked why by her perplexed mother, she had responded that the moon was happier there.

Mary found that the easiest thing was just to concentrate on the things she could control, and she happily went on pruning and deadheading and spraying her roses, a seemingly safe and fairly boring activity. During the summer in question, she was forced to spray even more than usual due to the humidity.

One fine summer afternoon, she had just started spraying her Blue Girl when she noticed something - something quick and silvery flitting at the back of the rose. A glint of sunshine touched an opalescent sliver of brightness which flung light back at her face like rain drops on a breeze. She gently pulled a branch toward herself and stared at the back of the bush. As she bent over, she felt a whirring above her head. Something brushed the back of her neck. With a little shriek, she leapt up and swatted at her collar. She felt a tendril of hair escape her careful bun. She followed the drone of wings to the back corner of the garden right next to the dense, ancient butterfly bush. The bush loomed huge and dark, reaching its intricate, leafy arms over the fence, a giant hairy old man; it certainly could be a breeding ground for giant insects. She stared at it warily.

She pulled back one of Auguste Renoir's branches to see if she could find the intruder. Perhaps it was just a large dragonfly. The iridescent light rippled onto the leaves in front of her. At first there was nothing, and then a sort of buzzing and...whack! Something hit her in the face and then buzzed away hovering about six to eight inches in front of her crossing eyes. When she uncrossed them, she had to look twice.

It was a fairy, just a bit bigger than her hand and brown as an acorn with leafy green hair and sharp green eyes. His nearly translucent wings were catching and flinging the sunlight in all directions. He was fluttering right in front of her. Her mouth dropped open briefly, and the soap bubble that surrounded her well established world quivered. It couldn't actually be a fairy, nevertheless it appeared to be a fairy. Mary tried to make sense of the illusion.

The apparition seemed to be glaring at her. He was wearing a loin cloth made out of what appeared to be a fresh petal from her Mr. Lincoln rose, which immediately annoyed her, illusion or not. He stared at her, continuing to hover about a foot in front of her nose. She had to back up to see him properly. His silvery wings whispered in the warm sunshine. The smell of cut grass and roses and Isabelle's mint and gardenia hovered thick in the air. He gazed intently at her, looking her up and down with a sour look on his little, pointed face.

Finally, he spoke. "Hey. Would you quit spraying poison on these roses?" He frowned and pointed his little finger toward her nose, poking it lightly with a sharp little finger nail. "It's drifting into the butterfly bush where we live. It's gross."

Mary realized that her mouth was hanging open. With an effort, she closed it. She continued to stare at the tiny creature. "I don't believe in fairies," she finally managed in a whisper.

The fairy sighed. He flew right up the bridge of Mary's nose and nearly made her go cross eyed again. He pulled out an eyebrow hair.

"Ouch!" yelled Mary.

Mary covered her eye with one hand and waved the other around the fairy.

"Okay lady," he said. "Do you believe in me now? Are you going to stop spraying that crap on the roses?" He narrowed his eyes, hovering intently in front of her, "Or not?"

She put her hands down and assessed the hallucination. The dream before her had all the sharpness of reality and the strange taste of truth, although one could not rationally assent to such a thing. She grasped for a way forward. If there were fairies...if there were fairies...well things couldn't go on as they were...she would have to spend her days blowing soap bubbles and playing in mud puddles and...and walking barefoot. She shook her head...what nonsense was filling it...why would she be forced to do any of those things. Fairies weren't real and why would they require her to remove her shoes? Her mind was filling with gibberish. Was she in a dream? Maybe she was dehydrated. Or in a fever. Perhaps she was in a hospital room in her former reality, unconscious. There were no fairies in that reality...but if there were...or if she were stuck in the wrong reality...then she would have to crawl out the window in the night to see the moon...just as Virginia did...she would be forced to go down to the river and let her hair down and put her feet in...and then she wouldn't have time for the things that she had to do...things like...like... oh...she couldn't remember them now.

The comfortable blanket of her life was slipping from around her thin, soft shoulders. She felt naked. Her life...she had one...just this morning she had a life and a history...

Had life always been about lying in a field looking at stars, smelling the dirt after the rain, feeling cat whiskers on her cheek? All that was left were a few odds and ends, memories that she didn't even know she had, memories that felt like they must have belonged to someone else once. The sweet, sharp taste of grass blades, a wobbly rainbow of oil in a puddle, the feeling of water under a boat, the full moon glittering across frost, the smell of a leaf fire, a puppy licking her foot, the silky feeling of skin on skin, the warmth of a kiss. That was all she could remember. Fragments and sensations. She looked up to see the fairy grinning like a devil at her. And suddenly she was angry. It wasn't fair. She was in the wrong world.

She thought hard...what was it...where had she come from? She wanted her own world back; she didn't like being naked in her thoughts in this other place. She took a deep breath, puffed out her cheeks and blew the thoughts of moon and river, cat whiskers and mud puddles right out of her mind and...Ah...there it was: a meeting at church; the flower show; a dinner party on Friday; her carefully mismatched china and the antique silver service. The ground that had been rocking and swelling under her like the water under a boat suddenly came to a trembling halt.

"I am not going to lose first place at the flower show due to an illusion," she said with her voice shaking. "Nor am I going to miss my meeting. I am fine, and this is not real." She leaned down to pick up the bottle of fungicide, meaning to put it back in her willow garden basket and then go inside and take an aspirin, although that might not have been clear to the fairy.

"Have it your way," said the fairy with a shrug. He shot up suddenly into the bright blue of the sky. Mary followed him with her eye until he disappeared into the hot, white light at the edge of the sun. She felt a moment of relief. It had been a hallucination and she had banished it by simply acting in a sensible manner. Remaining thoughts of soap bubbles, free flowing hair, puppies and bare feet fell away from her, absorbed by the thick green lawn. All her meetings and menus and hair appointments found room again.

And then she saw it, a tiny shape moving back out of the circle of the sun, small and dark, diving toward her like a kamikaze.

Mary automatically put up a hand to ward him off, but he slammed into her thumb, wrapped himself around it and bit her...hard. She felt the needlelike teeth pierce deep into her skin, all the way to the bone. His saliva flowed into her blood. It started at the tiny holes he had ripped in her flesh. Flaming hot at first, it penetrated her blood stream and shot through her, an arrow, a scorching head of fire trailing the icy tail of a comet so that first her blood boiled where it met the toxin then turned bitter cold behind it. The fire raced around her hand and up her arm. Then her arms and hands became too cold to move. The flame raced into her head, fairy venom slowly searching out every part of her from the inside. When the venom hit her chest, she was incapacitated. Her heart burst into a white-hot flame, then congealed. She fell backwards into the Double Delight, scratching her arms and bloodying her crisp white shirt, and then she lay there as the poison finished winding its way through, first burning then freezing her stomach, then her hips and legs. Every organ, every muscle was outlined in pain one fraction of an inch at a time, a revelation in anguish. The fairy venom searched out every last bit of her body, every molecule, every cell, until she felt its heat tracing the inside of her toes. Then she lay frozen and unmoving on the soft green grass with the sun above and the flowers shaking gently in the June breeze.

She was so cold that she could not even shiver. She thought briefly about death but found it uninteresting, and then for the first time in her life, she thought nothing. A flower petal fell gently on her face as though she did not exist. June and warmth and flowers and birds and bees dwelt in the earth around her, but she was nothing...a cold hole in the universe.

Mary was found on her lawn by Father Dingle because she missed a church committee meeting for the first time in her life. She then spent four days completely insensible in Whistlestop Memorial Hospital with a bizarre ailment that mystified her doctors. Anyone who has lived in a small town will understand the strange mix of sympathy, curiosity, and secret gratification involved in such a serious and alarming occurrence. While the excitement lasted, Mary's family was knee deep in casseroles and gossip. However, just as the hearsay was reaching its pinnacle, and the organist was wondering whether to cancel her trip out of town for the funeral of the year, Mary sat up and asked the nurse for tea and toast. With a sigh of relief, and truth be told, a bit of disappointment that the fun was over, the town collected itself and went back to business.

Mary recovered her health rapidly and for a few weeks all was quiet. She told Bob and Virginia about her experience in the garden, although she couldn't be certain if it had really happened. She briefly seemed to be growing more lucid and healthy. Then the "incidents" began. About two weeks after her release, Mary was found in the park in a thin silk nightgown halfway up the giant oak at 6:00 AM, apparently talking to a squirrel. Bob was there along with the fire department. Everyone was trying to talk her down but to no avail. Mary refused to leave the tree until noon and was quite bellicose with Bob, Fire Chief Marsh, and the squirrel.

The next week a pair of kayakers found her with unkempt hair, clad in only her underwear, singing an aria from Ophelia's mad scene sitting on a log overhanging the river. By the time Bob and the constable arrived, she had drifted away. Ultimately, she was found in a deep sleep on her back-porch swing still in her underwear.

Within two days of the river incident, Mary Jo Baker called Bob from the diner on the square to tell him that Mary was riding a bike around town in the hot sun. She was wearing one of Virginia's costume cloaks and she had wrapped all her jewelry around her neck and head. She was telling people that she was a Berber and she had just returned from the desert. Bob managed to talk her into going home by promising to think about purchasing a camel. This went against his plain and practical way of dealing with things but seemed preferable to the continued humiliation of his wife's very public decline.

Sheriff Henry called Bob only a few days later to ask him if he knew that Mary and Homeless Tom were having "wine tastings" in the park with some bottles from Bob's wine collection and some of Mary's antique wine glasses. Bob did not. He was also rather surprised on pulling up to retrieve his wife and his wine to discover Mary in one of her best evening gowns, complete with opera gloves. Homeless Tom was wearing one of Bob's silk ties.

Bob was beginning to think that he would soon be as unhinged as Mary with all the worry she was causing him. The townsfolk were beginning to think that Mary was more entertaining than she had ever been, dinner parties be damned. Virginia was beginning to think she had underestimated Mary on some level, somehow. And Elwin McGee, the fairy who had bitten her in the first place, was beginning to think he had gone too far. The rapid progression of symptoms disturbed him.

As the incidents increased in volume and sheer weirdness, it became apparent that Mary needed supervision. That task fell to Virginia. Surprisingly, much of her time with her mother that summer was unexpectedly pleasant. Virginia had never particularly enjoyed unstructured time with Mary before.

Virginia took her mother to Isabelle's garden and they fed the fish in the shallow koi pond and told them mermaid stories. They went to the lake together, and Virginia listened to her mother sing snatches of opera, for which Mary had trained as a young girl. They rowed a flat-bottomed boat toward a grassy island for picnics. They had tea parties and pretended to hunt unicorns. Virginia taught her to paint. They threw rocks at trains, stayed out all night, gazed at stars, made poems for the moon. Mary was convinced that a colony of feral cats behind an abandoned house worshipped her as their goddess; when this feeling overtook her, she brought them cat food, and, while they ate, she made grand pronouncements with one of Virginia's old princess crowns on her head. They picked flowers, danced in the rain, and made old fashioned lemonade.

But things did not remain so pleasant. Mary's mind tilted wildly. She seemed destined to slide out of control, through some dark door in the universe. Virginia tried to explain the situation to Bob but to no avail. If Mary wasn't in trouble, he wasn't interested. It was the only way he could stay sane. He had important work to do at the bank and surely Virginia could see that they needed to eat. If no police or authorities were involved, then Bob could put it out of his mind and get on with life.

Virginia didn't have this luxury. Mary seemed to be moving further and further away from them and toward some shadow that only she could see. Once, on one of their wild moonlit nights, Virginia had to pull Mary from the river.

"I'm going with the river," Mary said from the dark water. "I want to feel it licking at my skin." She lay on the water as though she were going to bed and began to sink. Virginia saw her, pale with moonlight, smiling as the water tugged at her clothes and hair, soothingly sucking her into its liquid darkness.

"You'll drown," said Virginia. But Mary didn't hear or didn't care. Virginia waded into the water and dragged her mother back to shore.

Another time, Mary found the sharp edge of a broken bottle glinting in the grass and before Virginia could take if from her, she had cut her finger. She was staring at it, watching the blood fall in droplets to the ground.

"It bit me," said Mary simply, "That's good."

She seemed enchanted by the blood droplets that fell from her hand and she swirled them onto her other hand and made patterns on her shirt.

Virginia had no reply. She buried the shard in the dirt and took her mother home to clean her up.

Even in the grip of her newfound affection for her mother, Virginia found it to be a difficult summer. Eventually, she could no longer take Mary out in the boat. Her mother was drawn like a magnet to depths of the lake. She tried to climb out of the boat to be swallowed by the deep, dark belly of water. That was that. Once, Virginia narrowly managed to pull her mother from the edge of a cliff on a hike. Mary became enamored with the motion and rush of the trains, and Virginia feared she would be lost in the mighty rush of the wheels.

Virginia was at a loss. Bob couldn't afford to think about it; the townsfolk began to say quietly with a shake of the head that things couldn't go on like this. Elwin McGee sat in his butterfly bush thinking and thinking. It didn't usually go this far. A fling, running naked through the park, eating a little dirt or otherwise committing embarrassing acts when the wildness flowed into your blood were all symptoms certainly, but they eventually wore off. Those things happened. This was different; he had never seen someone so affected by the bite. He'd never seen a human with no immunity at all.

Virginia had taken to tucking her mother into bed in the guest room across the hall from her own bedroom, so she could keep an eye on her. One night in the late summer, Mary tired early. By ten o'clock, she seemed to be in a deep slumber. But Virginia was too accustomed to late hours and wild nights. She was bone tired but somehow too restless to sleep. After about half an hour of hopeless tossing and turning, she looked out to see the moon rising. She threw on an old, soft jacket and headed out. She swung herself easily over the picket fence and sat in the shadows of Isabelle's garden, letting the moonlight pour down on her face.

She was attempting to let the moon soothe her into sleepiness when she heard something on the other side of the bush. She crept close to the fence and peered through. There was Mary. She was standing in the corner of the yard next to the August Renoire in a thin silk nightgown. It was a chilly night, but she was not shivering. She stood calmly as though she were waiting for something. Virginia strained closer. She crouched under the butterfly bush on Isabelle's side of the fence. She felt the bush vibrate and she heard the fluttering of leaves. She looked up, startled. There were hundreds of tiny lights above her, glimmering and moving through the branches.

Mary stood very still, watching. The lights gathered themselves into a glittering sphere. The orb moved from the bush and hovered over Mary's head. One light separated itself and hovered in front of Mary's face. Virginia squinted. The light was emanating from a tiny person. A person with wings.

"Mary?" the tiny person asked.

"I am glad you bit me," said Mary. "But I don't think I can stay here anymore."

"I expect not," said Elwin. "You had no immunity. I didn't know."

Mary nodded.

"Would you like to lie down?" asked the tiny man. "I expect it would be more comfortable...as such things go."

"Okay," said Mary. She lay gently on the ground on her side. She arranged her gown.

"Elwin?" said Mary softly.

"Yes?" he asked

"I'm sorry. About the roses I mean," a single tear caught the moonlight.

"It's okay, Mary. I'm sorry too," he said.

She said, "I'm ready," and she smiled and wiped away the diamond tear.

Elwin darted up and rejoined the ball of light. It hovered and hummed a moment and then swelled. The giant light moved up in the air, like a zeppelin taking flight and then dove. The light swallowed Mary. Virginia heard a cry of joy and pain and then saw nothing but the humming of the light. At first, Virginia could see the outline of her mother's body in the swarm of light. Then the light became even lighter, whiter, transparent. Mary was gone. Virginia gasped and then sat perfectly still with her back against the fence, just breathing. The moon poured its cold sympathy down on her, shining, shining on the living and the dead - as it always does.

Virginia was startled to find Elwin hovering in front of her.

"Hey kid," he said.

Virginia stared at his chin. She pointed to her own chin and made a tiny wiping motion. Elwin flicked out his tongue and licked off the tiny speck of blood.

"I'm sorry," he said.

"Yeah," Virginia said. She couldn't think of anything else to say.

Elwin scratched his head. "I'm not sure what I can do for you to make up for things, but I can give you this," he said. He darted forward and kissed her forehead. She felt a terrible, beautiful warmth filling her. She opened her mouth to say something, anything, and then tasted moonlight as it fell on her tongue. She heard flowers growing next to her. She felt the movement of the ground beneath her as the earth spun its orbit around the sun and she felt the universe expanding until it slid aimlessly into other universes.

She split into more than one Virginia and then reformed herself. Elwin was smiling at her.

"You'll be fine I think," said Elwin. "Moonlight gets in your blood."

She sat quietly in the garden staring at Elwin for a second and then tried her feet. The earth was still moving but she took to it like a natural born sailor takes to walking on a boat in the ocean.

"Thanks then," she said.

"No problem," said Elwin.

Virginia went upstairs and packed her knapsack. She was gone by morning. Bob did not see her again for many years, when she resettled in the town, a famous and well-traveled artist. Most of the townsfolk assumed that she had taken Mary away to keep Bob from putting her in an institution. A few of them suspected Bob of foul play, but he doggedly went about his business, refusing to respond to any of the rumors. Eventually, he married one of the bank tellers. She was young and pretty, and she threw magnificent dinner parties.

A Snake in the Grass

Butterflies lifted and landed and lifted again, trying to get the last of the nectar from each flower before Alma discarded it. She was in her flower garden weeding and deadheading furiously. It was out behind the kitchen garden, way behind the house where no one could see her angry tears. Truth be told, she liked to deadhead flowers when she was annoyed, and today she was steaming. Her sister-in-law had decided to have her daughter's engagement party on the third weekend of September, when Alma always, always had her family over for Joe's birthday.

That weekend had been Joe's weekend every year since they'd been married. He'd been dead now for three years, and she still had his party because it made her feel close to him, gave the kids and grandkids a way to remember him. As an added benefit, she could remind the kids that she was a lonely old widow who could do with more company. Joe's sister, Sally, and his nieces and nephews and cousins always came. Alma's own brother was far and away up in Michigan now, but even he tried to come when he could. Everyone knew what that weekend meant to her. They knew how hurt she would be if she couldn't have her party. And here was Sally. Taking her weekend. It was the only weekend they could reserve the country club, Sally said. The only weekend the groom's family and everyone else could come, Sally said. In the hurry and bustle of planning, she'd just forgotten that this was Joe's weekend, Sally said. Couldn't Alma have her party another weekend?

Of course, that wasn't the only time Sally had hurt Alma's feelings. When Joe was alive, she was always asking him to come and do this or that, taking up his weekends, time that should have been spent with Alma and the kids. Sally's husband was the richest man in town. Still, she was always asking Joe to come over and give her advice on this or that, or to fix some little something for her.

Then there were the gifts. How many times had Sally bought one of Alma's kids something lavish for Christmas? Something she knew good and well Alma and Joe couldn't afford. She'd taken each of Joe and Alma's kids to Europe when they graduated. Joe had given his permission, said the travel was a wonderful opportunity. Must be nice to have enough money to buy affection from your family and friends. Sally had been eight years younger than Joe and he'd always spoiled her, like the rest of the family.

Alma snapped heads off three zinnias at once, startling some drowsy bumble bees into flight. She was trying to get hold of herself, but Lord was she mad. Sally always could make Alma feel like a little nobody. Now maybe, maybe, like Joe had always said, she wasn't trying to make anyone feel that way, maybe she was just a happy go lucky girl who'd always managed to land on her feet, and she wanted to share her good fortune. Maybe she just called Joe because she wanted an excuse to see him. But if Sally had been paying attention, she would have seen how she made Alma feel all these years. Apparently, she never had.

Alma stood up. Then she bent over and struck at some crab grass beside the zinnia bed. That stuff was always trying to crawl right in with the flowers. She hit it sharp and hard with her little garden knife, pulled the clump out and flung it. Here she was letting Sally ruin her day again. How many times had that happened since she and Joe married? And Sally never even seemed to notice when she hurt Alma and made her feel bad. She always made out like she and Alma were the best of friends.

The hot weather and hard work were starting to take the edge off Alma's stress when she heard a rustling in that last row of zinnias, the stripy ones she was so proud of. It was a steady sound of movement low on the ground. Deaf as she was, she knew that sound. A snake, sure as the devil went to Eden.

Her muscles tightened, and her heart pounded before she even caught sight of the snake. Her stomach tied itself into a hard knot. Unfortunately, what Alma had gained in wisdom, she'd lost in reflexes. Her fight or flight impulses were shriveled with age so the synapses in her brain froze her knobbly knees into place instead of sending her legs running. Before she could get control of herself, the snake appeared right at her feet.

She stood still, steeled herself to remain calm. Her hoe was in the barn. She could only hope that instead of striking her, the snake would move off.

To her surprise, the snake did neither of those things. This was not a common black snake. Instead its skin was a delicate apricot color. The strong sunlight caused it to glisten into iridescence. Alma was barely breathing. If only the snake would take no notice of her. But it slowly lifted its head and fixed copper color eyes on her own. She could not look away. The serpent's tongue flicked in and out a few times. It seemed to be thinking. Then slowly, lifting from the tail, the snake undulated and rose level with her own head, looking straight into her eyes. Alma thought she might pass out with fear.

"Close your mouth, Alma," the snake said in a soft whispery voice. "You look very silly."

It stared into her eyes, head moving back and forth rhythmically. Alma found her own head swaying. She could not break the serpent's hypnotic gaze. She felt fear in the rational part of her brain, but to her surprise her body began to relax. Her heartbeat slowed, her breathing became deeper and the knot in her stomach loosened.

She closed her mouth. She finally managed to move her own eyes away from the hypnotic gaze, instead she found herself dazzled by glowing apricot skin. As much as she hated snakes, its skin was like the petals on the peachy, golden rose that hung over her arbor. Alma found herself surprised by a sudden impulse to stroke the soft, silken body. The compulsion frightened her. She thrust her hands behind her back.

"Good thinking Alma, smart, very smart," said the serpent, "It's best not to touch me. Do you know why Alma?"

The snake was speaking but Alma could not form words. Her mouth opened and shut without result. The snake still hovered in front of her, only its very lower body touching the ground.

"It's alright Alma," said the snake, "I know you're startled. I sympathize. I'm very sympathetic. Now answer my question."

"I'm sorry," Alma finally croaked out, "What was the question?"

"Do you know," hissed the snake, "Why it's best not to touch me?"

"No," Alma said.

"Because," the serpent said, "I bite."

"Oh," said Alma, "I see."

"No," said the snake, "I don't think that you do. But that's all right. I probably won't bite you. Do you know why?" Once again, Alma was distracted by an overwhelming urge to touch the snake's shimmering skin.

"I asked if you knew why I probably wouldn't bite you," said the snake, their noses nearly touching now.

"No. No, I don't. Why?" Alma said finally. "Why won't you bite me? And how do you know my name?"

"Now that's more to the point Alma," said the snake, "You should be asking questions. For heavens sakes. Of course. Here I am in your garden like I belong, and you've never seen me before. I know your name. It's only right to question me. Now, I will answer one of your questions. The other you might think over for yourself. I probably won't bite you because I like you, Alma."

"I see," said Alma.

"Come," said the serpent, "I am not at my most comfortable in this upright position. I don't know what you humans see in it. Let's go to the garden bench."

Alma walked obediently to the small cedar bench at the edge of the cut flower garden, the one Joe had made for her the year before he died, with the snake slithering alongside her feet like a loyal dog, though she felt more like the snake's obedient pet. When she sat down, it raised itself up and slid headfirst onto her lap, long, muscled body pulling up slowly next to her, tail coiled around the leg of the bench. It was surprisingly heavy.

"I thought I wasn't supposed to touch you," Alma said.

"You're not," said the snake, "I'm touching you. It's entirely different."

"I see," said Alma. She gripped the bench seat to keep herself from stroking the soft, smooth skin. The sound of a crow cawing overhead sounded like a warning. But what could she do? She closed her eyes and tried to concentrate on the smell of cut grass and the slight breeze that evaporated the sweat from her forehead. But all she could think of was the feeling of the heavy snake stirring slightly against her legs.

"You want to touch me, don't you," said the snake. It rubbed the arrow shaped head along her leg and nudged itself into her soft old belly. A strange tingling slid down her thigh and into her chest, "You can if you want. As I said, I probably won't bite you."

The sun felt heavy and warm, pressing her down against the bench. The weight of the massive snake on her lap kept her from rising and she realized, oddly, she didn't want to. A musky fragrance and something else – maybe tuberose and honeysuckle she thought – rose as the heat of the sun warmed its body. Almost without permission of herself, her hand slid up touching smooth, apricot skin.

Instantly, the head flicked around. Teeth caught her hand. Alma squealed.

"I said probably, Alma. Probably. Anyway, that was a love bite, just instinct. Check your skin, I doubt I even broke it," the snake settled itself comfortably on her lap again.

To be sure, Alma found two tiny scratches, but her skin was whole.

"Now that I think about it Alma, that was lovely," said the snake, "Please stroke me again."

"I'm afraid," replied Alma. Her hand hovered above the serpent's back.

"Rightly so, rightly so," said the snake. "Nevertheless, now that I've shown you that I can bite, you should be just as frightened to disobey me by not petting me, especially as I am lying across your lap. And not only can I bite, I can crush."

The snake unwound itself from the bench and rolled its tail around her leg and squeezed, just to give her a little taste of what it felt like to be crushed.

Alma looked down at the silky glistening skin and let the musky, sweet smell fill her head. Against her better judgement she found herself once again stroking the heavy body. The snake rubbed against her belly and pushed against her hand, soft as silk, smooth as cream. At long last the animal pulled back from her hand.

"You may stop, Alma," it said.

It slid up her body, resting its head on her breasts. It gently moved aside the neckline of her dress with its head and she felt the tongue on her collarbone, flickering against her skin.

"Thank you," the snake said, "Now let us speak frankly with one another. You have been kind to me, perhaps I can do something for you."

"What could you do for me?" Alma asked. A light breeze touched the sweat on her neck and gave her a little chill. She heard the crows caw again. She looked up to see one circling and settling on a big oak tree, watching to see how things would come out.

"Well," said the snake, "I can bite. Perhaps you have enemies."

"What do you mean?" asked Alma, "I'm a churchgoing woman. I would never have you bite someone. No sir. That isn't right."

The snake pulled itself away from her body to look her in the eye, red tongue flashing out to touch her nose. "Oh Alma. You can talk to me. I know. I understand."

It began to caress her chin.

It slid up to her ear and lightly touched the inside, flickering and tickling with its tongue. Alma closed her eyes and pulled back from the snake a little.

"Remember Alma, I could have hurt you, but I didn't. I'm not wicked. If I bite someone, it's always for the best. My bite makes people better. My bite is repentance."

The snake rubbed its head on her neck, then dipped and flicked its tongue on her inner elbow. A bird chirped loud and anxious from the pole beans.

"Sometimes, people need to learn lessons Alma," it said. "And that's what my bite does, it teaches lessons."

Alma could hardly focus. "In Sunday school they said we should pray for our enemies, try to do good to them. I've always tried to do that. I can't imagine asking a snake to bite your enemy falls into that category."

She dug back through her mind to her days teaching Sunday School. She found she had a rather loose grip on the teachings of the church in that instant, "I'm afraid I can't ask you to bite someone."

"I'm the answer to those prayers for your enemies Alma," responded the snake. Its voice reverberated in her head like her own thought. "My bite is not exactly toxic; my bite makes people realize when they've done something wrong. You can't repent if you don't know when you've done something wrong."

Alma felt the splintered bottom of the old bench biting into her thin legs through the cotton dress, but she dared not complain.

"Let me explain," the snake said in a kindly tone. It stopped rubbing her for a moment and hovered in front of her, face-to-face, "If someone took something, my bite might help them understand they were wrong and return the stolen property. Or say someone had upset someone else. Perhaps with unkind words. My bite could make a person understand that he or she had been unkind and apologize. How many people simply can't see that they're wrong about something? My bite could cure that. When I bite someone, it's really a sort of good deed. Of course, some small amount of pain is necessary for repentance. Surely, there is someone who has wronged you. Someone you would like me to bite."

Alma was thinking hard, trying to find her way back through her foggy memory to her Bible. She tried to break free of the snake's logic. A rabbit scurried through the tomatoes in Alma's peripheral vision. She heard a truck on the road. Her brain picked at the loose ends and found a scrap.

"The snake in the garden of Eden was wicked," she finally managed.

"Of course," said the snake. "And all snakes were punished for that. Once someone's been punished we have to let it go, don't we Alma? Snakes have done our time so to speak. That's why we've been sent out into the world to bite. To make amends."

"I suppose," said Alma. "I suppose."

"What that first wicked snake did was to show Adam and Eve the difference between good and evil. It was a terrible thing to do Alma. Alas, what's done is done. Some things can't be reversed" said the snake, "In fact, since the Fall, religion is about knowing the difference between good and evil, wouldn't you say? Understanding evil and repenting."

"I suppose," said Alma. A hummingbird skimmed over her head to the jasmine on the arbor. She tried to follow it with her eye but was drawn to the gaze of the snake again.

"Why, what are sermons for if not to help you know the difference between good and bad?" asked the snake.

"That's true," Alma had to agree.

"Once my ancestor had let the cat out of the bag Alma, repentance became necessary, do you see? Once humans had knowledge of good and evil, they couldn't unlearn it. Repentance is what I'm offering.

One bite and a person will know they've been in the wrong. It won't hurt too much. Not really. Now...I know there's someone. I'm sure there must be," said the snake. "Someone that needs to know that they've done wrong. So, they can repent Alma."

Alma sat still under the blue sky. It was so quiet that she could almost hear the clouds. She glanced nervously at the back of her neat little brick house, even though she knew there was no one in it who could see what she was doing. The washing fluttered slightly in the breeze. It seemed absurd to be sitting on the garden bench talking religion with a snake.

The snake slid around Alma's body again and kissed her nose and under her chin with a flick of its tongue. She closed her eyes and it lightly licked her eyelid. Finally, she let out a long breath of pleasure that ended in a whisper, "Sally."

The snake immediately fell from her body and slithered to the ground. "I thought so," it said.

"Now Alma," said the snake, "There's one more thing you can do for me."

"Please don't bite anyone on my account," Alma said, "I'll help you any way I can, but please don't bite someone because of me. Don't bite Sally."

"You said her name, Alma," the snake replied. "I asked for a name and you gave me one. Now you just sit there for just one minute. I'll be back."

It slid to the edge of the zinnia bed and then turned, "It's alright Alma. It never hurts anyone to repent. Much."

Rippling into the zinnias, the snake disappeared. Flowers and leaves rustled for a moment and then all was quiet. Alma thought that she'd dreamed everything. She so fervently hoped it was a dream that she started to rise from the bench to collect her garden tools when she heard rustling.

The serpent's mouth was carefully stretched around a small oval. The glittering object rolled onto the grass. A tiny golden egg lay at Alma's feet.

"Here Alma," said the snake. "I need you to take this egg with you everywhere you go. Keep watch over my offspring until it hatches."

Alma bent down to retrieve the fragile, glittering object. She thought she could feel the tiny egg quivering slightly in her hand.

"It's tougher than it looks, Alma," the snake said. "Still, wrap it carefully. Always keep it with you. Put it in your purse if you have to run errands. You don't have to sit home and moon over it. But you must watch over it until it hatches, else I may have to become very, very irritable."

The snake flicked its tail as a warning.

"If I do, will you promise not to bite Sally?" Alma asked.

"I'll think about it," said the snake. "But really, repentance is very good for humans. You must do this thing for me though Alma, or really I will have to return and if I do, I will bite you."

Before Alma could say anything in response, the snake slipped away. Zinnias swayed, and the startled hummingbird shot skyward. She put the little egg in the pocket of her flowered dress, then she plopped down on the grass right in front of the zinnia bed and put her head in her hands. She was shaking. Purple, orange and bright pink zinnias quavered in the breeze. Butterflies still lifted and landed. The humming bird buzzed past her ear, but the serpent had driven the peace from the garden. The bright colors seemed sinister now. Alma didn't have the strength to go back to the house. She lay down on the grass and fell asleep. When she woke, purple twilight had started to settle. She made her way back inside the neat, empty house where she went straight to bed without saying her prayers.

When she woke next morning, Alma remembered everything and rejected it. Not possible. But there was the tiny golden egg on her night stand. She stood before it. Had it quivered? She held it in her hand and felt a tiny vibration. When she held it to her ear, it hummed. She wrapped the tiny egg in tissue paper and put it in a cardboard jeweler's box. Alma kept the egg with her day and night. At night, she slept with it on her night stand and all day she carried it from room to room with her. If she went out, she tucked it into her purse. At first, she didn't go out much, but she remembered that the snake had told her to live her life as usual. Besides, she certainly didn't want to explain to the kids that she couldn't go out because she was hatching a snake egg! Or have them hovering over her because they thought she was sick. No sir, explaining herself was not something she felt up to. She tried to go about her business so as not to raise suspicions.

She heard from Sally once or twice about the wedding. Sally was pretending to ask her advice about flowers or food for the reception or some such nonsense. Sally had caterers and florists. There was no reason to pretend she needed Alma around. Sally made no mention either of being bitten by a snake or feeling particularly sorry that she'd wronged Alma.

Alma began to feel almost silly. Maybe the snake had forgotten about her and Sally altogether. At any rate, it had said it would consider not biting Sally if Alma kept the egg. Sometimes she thought that she'd dreamed the whole thing, that she'd found the little egg after waking, and here she was, a foolish old woman carrying around an Easter decoration.

She couldn't quite convince herself that it wasn't true though, so one Wednesday evening she found herself carrying a purse with the little jeweler's box nestled inside to choir practice. Alma made her way down the basement stairs to the choir room and carefully placed her purse under her chair on the choir riser. About midway through practice, she noticed it had scooted itself forward just a bit. By the end of practice, she could feel her purse moving and vibrating just a little under her leg. She bent down and made sure it was zipped tight. She took off her sweater and draped it over the seat of her chair. She was sweating.

She almost jumped out of her skin when the purse slid forward and made contact with her calf while she was talking to Mary Jo Baker about the Fall Festival. The Home Circle Ladies had promised to handle the bake sale. Mary Jo went on at some length about how much easier it was to sell cookies and cupcakes, how last year people brought whole pies and cakes. Then the ladies had to cut and sell single slices at the end of the sale, which Mary Jo thought was messy and wasteful. She also wondered whether Mrs. Harrison should be discouraged from her caramel cake because it was sticky at first, but then the icing always dried to dirt colored dust before they could sell it. Alma's heart almost jumped through her mouth three times, trying to answer Mary Jo, not knowing what was going on inside her purse. Afterwards, she couldn't have told anyone what she'd promised to bring to the bake sale for a million dollars. But she bravely babbled on about the impossibility of selling oatmeal cookies with raisins and the need to firmly tell the Smith woman no more weepy meringue tarts because the church reception hall was too hot, all the while with that quivering purse under her chair.

After talking with Mary Jo, she sat there until the choir room cleared out, pretending to mark her music. Only Alan Cunningham, the choir director, and Myrtle Anderson, the accompanist, were left. They were standing by the door talking about Sunday's service. She reached under her chair to quickly wrap her purse in her sweater, so she could sneak out the back stairs when she saw her chance.

It was then that she realized that her purse had a hole in the side. And peering out was a small apricot snake.

"Oh dear," Alma squeaked.

"Alma? What is it?" asked Myrtle. Alan and Myrtle turned to look at her.

"I...errr...nothing," said Alma. They went back to their conversation.

Alma slid the sweater back over the purse, only to find a little arrow shaped head pushing it aside to look at her.

"Thanksssss," it said in a whisper.

Alan and Myrtle looked up at Alma again.

"Oh dear! Who's that at the door!" said Alma, gesturing wildly at the choir room door. Myrtle and Alan turned their heads and in an instant the snake shot out from under Alma's sweater. It made directly for the supply closet door behind the piano and slithered right underneath.

"I don't see anyone," Alan said, pulling his head back inside. "Are you sure you heard something Alma?"

"Oh sorry!" Alma said. "I guess I was wrong."

Alan shrugged, "Myrtle and I are going to dig a couple of anthems out of the music library. Lock the door when you leave, will you?"

"Oh certainly," Alma said. "I'm leaving in just a second. Just wanted to finish marking this music. Hit a few wrong notes. Mind if I take my folder home?"

"No, just sign it out. And bring it back please. I don't have the budget to keep replacing folders," Alan and Myrtle left the room.

Alma bounced down the choir risers, snagging her sweater on a chair. She ran to the supply closet. She opened the door and peered in. There was an apricot tail sticking out of a slender hole in the concrete. Dust was flying. The tiny snake appeared to be drilling into the foundation of the church. She stood staring for just a second and saw the little arrow-shaped head pop back up briefly. The tiny snake gazed at her.

"Thanksss again," it said. "You can be on your way. I'm fine."

Alma could have sworn it winked at her. Then it disappeared into the hole. Alma stood staring at the tiny opening for a few minutes wondering what, if anything, she could do. Not a thing, she finally decided. She moved the mop bucket over the hole.

She picked up her purse and unzipped it. She saw tissue paper and cardboard shredded into confetti. The snake had eaten through the box and then the purse. She wrapped her sweater around her purse, put her choir folder under her arm and locked the choir room door.

She was making her way to the back stairs when Father Dingle came puffing around the corner.

"Oh Alma, is that you? Oh dear," Father Dingle caught her arm. "I thought I saw your car outside. Your daughter called."

He looked flustered and cleared his throat a time or two, "She asked me to catch you if only I could."

He pushed his glasses up off his round cheeks. His face was a little red and his forehead was shining with sweat. He began to murmur, "Oh dear, Oh dear."

He guided her upstairs, his hand on her elbow. Alma was puzzled.

"Alma would you like to sit down for a second?" He led her into the sanctuary where most of the lights were already off. He steered her into a dimly lit pew in the front of the church.

"Alma, your children called. Alice to be exact. But the others were there too. Oh dear. They wanted me to tell you that…" Father Dingle trailed off and then reached forward and patted Alma's hand. "That Sally is dead."

"Dead?" Alma asked. "How can Sally be dead?"

"I'm sorry," Father Dingle said. He patted her hand again. Alma flung it away.

"How could that happen?" Alma asked. "She was in perfect health. She was fine. She shouldn't be dead."

"It was very odd," Father Dingle said, his hands fluttering over hers. "Her daughter found her in the summer house. She was already gone I'm afraid. The doctor thought it might be some sort of snake bite."

He pulled a Kleenex out of his pocket, offering it to her.

"I understand the snake bite!" Alma cried out. "I don't understand how she's dead! She shouldn't be dead!"

Reverend Dingle fumbled with her hand for a moment, "I'm sorry Alma, I know how shocking this must be. I know how close you were. Please let me drive you to the hospital. The family is waiting for you."

Alma looked up into the dark arch of the church where the last of the summer light flickered eerily through the stained-glass pictures of Jesus on the mount. A ray of light pierced the glass eye of the Savior and went straight into her chest. She gasped for breath.

"I didn't mean her to die," Alma whispered. She held Father Dingle's hand tightly. "You know I would never kill anyone Father Dingle? I told the snake not to bite her." Alma was trembling. "I didn't do this father. The snake...Lord help. I didn't do it!"

Father Dingle's eyes were wide. He tried to pat her hand, but she pushed him away.

"The snake tricked me Father! I was tricked! The same old serpent that tricked Eve. Oh, help me Father! Help me Jesus!" She buried her head in her hands and sobbed and shook, "Please believe me. This isn't my fault. And I had to release the snake in the basement, the little one. What could I do? Lord help!"

"Oh dear!" Father Dingle said. He began to look around the darkened sanctuary. He squirmed a little on the wooden pew, "Perhaps I can get you some water. Are you alright? Oh dear!"

"I couldn't help it! I couldn't. The snake was rubbing against me, it made me feel so nice Father. And the scent of it! You would have said her name too! Anyone would!" Alma cried out. She grabbed Father Dingle's hands so tightly that he winced.

"Oh, my goodness!" said Father Dingle. He tried loosening his fingers from hers, but Alma gripped them tighter.

She sobbed, "Forgive me, Father!"

Father Dingle shoved another Kleenex at her and yanked his hand out of hers.

"Oh dear! Oh dear!" Sit there for just one second, Alma," Father Dingle said. He ran to the sanctuary door.

"Alan!" he called out. "Myrtle? Anyone?"

Alma couldn't remember much about the funeral nor afterwards for a time. She couldn't remember much of what she'd said to anyone about the snake or about Sally. Those first few weeks were a fog. After talking with Father Dingle and then listening to their mother, her children had called Dr. Ford. After listening to Alma for around ten minutes, Dr. Ford had insisted on the pills. She slept a good deal. She supposed that was what the pills were meant to do. Keep her out of everyone's hair.

She had vague memories of being hustled away from Sally's casket at the funeral. And Alice had her husband Barry take Alma home after she'd tried to apologize to Sally's daughter. She had nebulous memories of her own grandchildren being shooed out of the room when she tried to explain what happened. All of life became indistinct. The only thing that seemed clear to Alma now was all the memories of Sally that came bubbling up, surprising her. The time Sally had leant her the cut glass punch bowl, the time Sally had bought them groceries when Joe's leg was broken, the time she took the kids, so Joe and Alma could take that trip out West. She knew it was too late, but she couldn't help trying to tell people about Sally. About how kind she had been. The children, who knew how Alma had always felt about Sally, huddled and decided it was definitely dementia.

Alma lived now in a haze of medicine and guilt. She learned not to talk about the snake at all. When they finally had to go back to their own lives, her children hired a middle-aged widow to stay with her. Alice took the keys to Alma's car. The widow lady nodded at anything Alma said, knitted in Alma's front room, held her peace and gave Alma her pills.

It was late September before Alma returned to her garden. Nights were becoming chilly, but no frost had yet fallen. Her zinnias were still in bloom, although they'd been somewhat neglected. Colorful flowers topped tall stalks that were turning brown. Dead flowers and seed pods gave the brightly colored flowers that were left a melancholy air, taunting them with the impending winter.

She sat on the bench watching the zinnias die. A few tattered, elderly butterflies lifted themselves and tottered around the ancient petals. Then she heard rustling. She didn't move. That snake could come and bite her for all she cared.

She closed her eyes for a moment and then she heard her name.

"Alma," whispered the voice. She opened her eyes to see the apricot colored serpent, up on its tail, eye level.

"You killed Sally," Alma said. "You said the bite wouldn't hurt. You said it wasn't toxic."

"I never said my bite wouldn't hurt," the snake replied. "I said it would lead to repentance. Of course, you have to live long enough to repent."

"Did she have time to repent before she died?" asked Alma. "Was it even necessary? Anyway, I asked you not to bite her, and I did you that favor."

"Oh Alma," said the snake, "The bite wasn't for her. It was for you. You're still, here aren't you? And you've repented, haven't you? Now you know how much you cared for Sally and how much she cared for you. I think the bite was good for you."

"You tricked me!" shrieked Alma. "I wish I had my hoe. I'd teach you a lesson."

"Careful Alma," said the snake. "I'm harder to kill than I appear."

"Go ahead," Alma said, "Bite me."

"Oh Alma," said the snake. "You're meant to live ever so much longer. Besides, I could never do that. I told you. I like you." The snake winked at her and slid away through the dying zinnias.

Father Dingle, Some Mice, and the Portal to Hell

Maybe it started with the mice. Maybe the exodus of mice was the first sign that there was something amiss in the church basement. The choir room had been plagued by mice for as long as Father Dingle had been there. Alan Cunningham, the choir director, had been belly aching about adequate storage for music since he'd been there. Father Dingle remembered Alan had nearly been in tears at a staff meeting after finding a mouse nest made with scraps of the Hallelujah Chorus. Alan found this situation neither economically nor spiritually tolerable. But the following year, early in the spring, church mice began moving out of the basement in droves. Father Dingle arrived at church one morning to find several families of mice scurrying up the basement stairs, down the hall towards the front doors. More mice appeared each morning, waiting to dash out as soon as the heavy wooden doors were opened.

One morning he found a mouse quivering on the window sill in his office. The poor thing was so paralyzed with fear that he'd been forced to ease it out the window and into a scraggly rosebush outside with the end of a pencil. He could not bring himself to otherwise dispose of the poor shivering animal.

The mass evacuation of mice conducted itself quietly up to a point. Father Dingle was incuriously grateful that the rodents were leaving. He chalked up the exodus to a minor miracle and mentioned his gratitude every evening in his prayers. But then there was that Sunday morning when pandemonium broke out in the choir loft during the opening hymn...

A bewildered and trembling mouse crawled into Bunny Beardsley's purse to escape the basement. Finding itself in strange new terrain, it ran up Bunny's arm when she reached into her purse for a Kleenex, leaving her in a state of near shock. Then the mouse ran across the pew, behind the sopranos, shot up Mary Jo Baker's choir robe, right up her neck and perched trembling on her chignon, provoking high pitched squeals from the sopranos and what must have seemed a fervent, spirit filled dance by Mary Jo.

First Tenor Harlan Smith's instincts took over and he swatted the rodent out of Mary Jo's hair. It flew up in a beautiful, acrobatic arc, soaring high over the pulpit. It landed on the organ keys and the organist, Myrtle Anderson, a victim of both the mouse and the cleaning lady's zealous over polishing of the organ bench, slid right off, landing on her posterior with a thump and a rather unfortunate and somewhat vulgar exclamation that echoed and bounced against the old church rafters. One could hardly blame her, but of course, some people had.

Father Dingle retrieved a bottle of flavored brandy when he returned to his study after the incident. He contemplated the conversation he would need to have with old Mrs. Flowers, the cleaning lady. He would need to visit Myrtle, who had probably broken her tailbone, and he supposed he needed to go and pay a visit to Bunny who'd nearly passed out after the incident. He shuddered as he remembered the sopranos gathering round to flail at her with church bulletins while Mary Jo went for a wet paper towel. By the time he'd thought the whole thing through, Father Dingle found himself holding an empty bottle.

After the mice cleared out, two packages of Sunday school material had disappeared from the church steps. The postman stoically declared he'd delivered them himself and left them right under the archway at 10:15 just like always; Margie, the church secretary, just as stoically declared that she had gone out at 10:20 to find absolutely nothing there. Reverend Dingle found himself smack dab in the middle of a mess with phone calls to the Post Office and the publishing company. Father Dingle hated to be in the middle of a mess. Then the alter linens disappeared. That little mystery prompted an hours' long search. Father Dingle found the linens sitting nicely folded on a church pew, fouled with a small smudgy handprint, as though the hand that made it had been dipped in ash.

Father Dingle nearly had to break up a fistfight among the ladies of the altar guild. Oh dear! That had required some sorting. His head hurt just thinking about it. Then the copy machine broke down in a spectacular manner. Margie stepped out to the restroom while the bulletins were printing and returned to find her printer choking on a paper jam. Before the incident was over, the office was filled with the smell of burning wires and the church was in need of a new printer.

One chilly spring Sunday a few weeks before Easter, parishioners filing past the somber marble angel guarding the tomb of Reverend Barnabus Fletcher Cook, first pastor of Whistlestop, noticed something unusual. The memorial was sporting devil horns, a pair of Ray Bans, and a Hitler mustache, all of which had apparently been super glued on. Sheriff Henry questioned all of the youth, to their immense and haughty indignation, and to the dismay of Father Dingle who couldn't imagine any of their teenagers committing such acts of nonsense.

The very next day, Father Dingle went into work a little bit late. He went around to the side door, not sneaking really, but he had hoped no one would note the time. And then Margie rounded the corner, nearly knocking him to the ground. Her red hair was falling around her face. Her usually pallid complexion was red and splotchy.

She was gasping out, "You're not going to believe it. You're not going to believe what they did!"

Father Dingle was taken aback, "Who? Did what now?"

"I don't know! No one knows!" Margie burst into tears.

She led him into the church and took him to the nursery door.

In thick green lines, someone had painted a huge and crudely drawn sea serpent, fangs dripping spots of red blood, mouth open. The creature hovered over a lighthearted mural of Noah's ark, massive mouth set to snap off Noah's head. The serpent coiled around the ark, dwarfing it. Perhaps this was mere vandalism. Father Dingle had seen vandalism before, though. Normally, it was merely anger and angst bubbling to the surface of the teenage brain, a vessel too weak to contain it. This wasn't like that. The art was primitive but had a raw power. The serpent's eye was on Noah but seemed to include Father Dingle in its malevolent, twinkling gaze as well.

That was yesterday. Yesterday now seemed like the Golden Days of yore. Because today had been Hell. Truth be told, he had started the morning with a brandy headache. Fine. He had to admit that. But he'd been sober, if a little worse for wear that morning. He would swear that on a stack of Bibles. When he arrived, he had been in full command of his faculties.

He was walking down the hall toward his office to call some painters to cover the sea serpent. His head ached and his shoulders were knitting themselves together with tension when he felt someone grab his elbow. He whirled around to face Alan, the choir director.

"Why would you sneak up on a man like that, Alan?" he yelped.

Alan tugged on his arm and darted away, yelling, "The basement! Come quick!"

Father Dingle followed. Margie popped her head out of her office at the commotion and ran after the men.

When Father Dingle rounded the corner behind Alan, wisps of sinuous green smoke were easing themselves up the basement staircase and coiling round the rails like the sea serpent from the nursery. They seemed to be emanating from the choir room.

"We've got to save the Easter music!" Alan was gone...leaping down stairs, taking them two at a time.

"Alan! Stop!" Father Dingle cried after him in vain. That's when his anxiety evolved suddenly and permanently into full grown fear.

It was an all-encircling fear, a snake eating its own tail. He was afraid of what he would find in the basement. He was also afraid of the disgrace of neglecting pastoral duty. He was not only afraid, he was afraid of being afraid. He was frozen for a moment, but the thought of the young and lovely Margie seeing him run like a frightened mouse from the basement flitted across his brain and propelled him through his terror to the bottom of the stairs. Alan had already made the turn into the choir room.

Father Dingle paused, his feet felt like lead. There was something emanating from the choir room, invisible, more unyielding than smoke, a something that pushed him away like an invisible hand. He peered around the corner and forced himself through the door.

"Alan! Forget the music!" he called.

Alan had already forgotten the music. He stood mesmerized in the center of the choir room, transfixed on the open supply closet. A steady stream of green mud with red streaks bubbled up from it, as though from a witch's cauldron, and spilled out onto the floor. Father Dingle's first thought was that there had been some sort of geothermal event. Was the church crumbling into the earth's core?

His second thought was that he had inadvertently purchased the LSD variety of frozen waffles because as he lurched forward to rescue Alan, he too became mesmerized. Out of the bubbling cauldron of red and green mud, improbably large bubbles grew like balloons. They floated past, caught on various objects and burst, releasing swirls of green smoke that fell and slithered away, out of the door, and up the stairs. The poisonous green bubbles were not all that kept Father Dingle's feet planted. An enormous green globule bulged on the lip of the simmering supply closet. Unlike the more translucent smoke-filled bubbles, this globe was thick and gelatinous. It was oily and oozing.

Father Dingle meant to move forward, to grab Alan's shoulder and run, but before he could make contact, the dreadful egg swelled up and popped!

It shot out tracers of slime like a goopy green firework. Some of it splashed up and landed on the men. As he wiped specks of slime from his face, Father Dingle saw it. The egg had hatched a foot-long, dark greenish-black creature, with wings – some awful, miniature admixture of human and reptile. The word imp came to mind. Its bat-like wings were streaked with deep crimson red. It stood blinking at the edge of the closet, shivering and spitting, flinging slime around the room. It shook its wings to dry them, let out a piercing shriek and flew up and around the choir room, skimming neatly over their heads.

"Alan!" yelled Father Dingle, "We have to get out of here!"

Alan looked blankly at Father Dingle. A splatter of green fell from his hair. Father Dingle had no choice. He slapped Alan. Hard.

"Hey! Ow!" Alan snapped out of his stupor.

"Let's go!" Father Dingle yelled.

Alan's eyes slid back towards the music cabinet for one last glance, like Lot's wife at Sodom.

"Bugger the Easter music Alan! Let's go!" Father Dingle bellowed. The two men ran for the door, sliding on green slime and choking on the snake-like wraiths of smoke that squirmed around them. As Father Dingle turned back to close and lock the door to the choir room, all that he could think to do under the circumstances, he noticed three new green eggs swelling from the bottom of the supply closet.

He hadn't handled things well from that point on. He had to admit that. None of them had. Who could be prepared for known reality to go careening out of orbit? It ought to have felt like a bad dream. It didn't. The whole thing had a three-dimensional sharpness and clarity. The three of them should have immediately left the grounds, reported the incident he supposed. Would anyone have believed them? And pray tell...to whom does one report imps? Or demons, as he now suspected. He thought, upon reflection, that a portal to Hell had somehow been opened in the church basement. How and by whom were questions beyond his ken.

They hadn't run for help though. For a few moments, the three of them stood outside the windows of the basement choir room peering in, trying to wrap their minds around the bizarre scene. Crimson and green mud lapped out and reached the first set of choir risers, by now seven of the small flying gargoyles were zipping around the room, screeching like pterodactyls. They ate everything they could find. One of them tore through a choir robe and swallowed shreds of fabric. One crunched a music folder, tearing quickly through leather and paper. One gnawed through one of the legs of the practice piano. One found a box of Easter music. It ate almost all the cardboard and frantically started shoveling down cantatas, chewing them with obvious fervor. After a few seconds, it belched a shower of confetti and started again on another box. Father Dingle noticed something else. Something disturbing. The creatures appeared to be growing larger and darker. They were now all between two and three feet long, solid tar black except for the deep crimson streaks on their wings.

Father Dingle watched as one of the creatures tried to swallow what appeared to be the G3 hand bell, a larger lower octave bell. Two of the imp's companions were working on the higher octaves with more success. The imp appeared to be trying to unhinge its jaw in an attempt to swallow the enormous bell. One of his companions noticed his distress and shot out a bony hand, pulled down the jaw and with a clang the entire hand bell disappeared.

"There goes the G3," Alan said miserably. He was also the hand bell director. Even as it was happening, Father Dingle knew that standing around the window watching all Hell break loose in the church basement wasn't an appropriate response.

The demons were in a perfect frenzy of eating. They shrieked, splashing in red and green mud, fighting over the gray sweater that Lavinia Jones always left draped over her chair until one of them snatched it up and vacuumed it into his wide mouth, starting with a sleeve. The piano listed badly to one side and the piano bench was mostly splinters. The imps reduced the music folder cubby to half its size in no time. Everyone gasped when one of the monsters began chewing a metal music stand. It ate Alan's score. Alan cried out in anguish as it too became confetti.

What to do? What to do? What to do? There was no frame of reference. Father Dingle didn't even know what had happened, much less how to stop it. He could only look on in horror. Surely a priest should be able to do something about an open portal to hell and a pack of demons, but Father Dingle didn't know what. He had never been a brave man and no heroic actions came to mind. In fact, no actions of any kind came to mind. He didn't even run. He was cowardly and stupid.

One of the imps looked up, straight at the window. It caught Father Dingle's eye with its own. It was a malevolent and twinkling gaze, just like the gaze of the sea serpent on the walls of the nursery upstairs. With a loud cry, the creature flung itself at the window. Glass splintered. Father Dingle had just enough time to throw himself on Margie and push her to the ground before the creature burst through the window and went rocketing past them. Alan flung himself down as well. They heard a chattering, shouting noise above their heads and more glass splintering. The imps flew free of the church, some landing in trees and some hopping and clambering among gravestones, flicking out their tongues and spitting. Father Dingle noticed for the first time how dark the sky had become, ragged and murky through the bare tree branches. A few drops of rain pelted down. The creatures squealed, whether with excitement or displeasure Father Dingle could not tell. They gathered in the large twisted maple in the center of the graveyard, a shrieking knot of bat wings.

Father Dingle lifted his head and once again caught the eye of one of the creatures. It gibbered and pointed at him, then put hands on hips squealing and bouncing. It flung down a shower of twigs, spewing out green spit. Father Dingle turned his face down again, and then carefully looked up out of the corner of his eye. His submissive posture seemed to mollify the demons. The rain began to come down more seriously. Father Dingle found that if he moved more than an inch or two, one or more of the little demons turned a baleful eye in his direction and began spitting and throwing things.

"Keep still!" he hissed to Margie and Alan.

His bald head was getting wet. It occurred to him that his glasses would soon be almost useless as rain streamed over his head. Nevertheless, moving now was out of the question. Perhaps they could wait the creatures out.

"We have to get out of here!" Alan hissed back. "I can't stay here any longer. We have to get out of here!"

Alan's voice trembled. Father Dingle glanced at him through the mud, over the top of his foggy glasses. Alan was pale. He was breathing heavily. He was going to crack.

"Hush!" Margie whispered back, urgently. "Be still like Father Dingle says."

"We can't just stay here forever. We can't!" Alan whispered, his voice crackling and warbling. Suddenly he shrieked, "Somebody has to do something."

Father Dingle saw Alan raise himself up to his knees. Alan shook his fist. He picked up a rock.

"No! Alan!" Father Dingle hissed.

Margie reached over to tug at his pant leg, "Alan! Stop!"

But Alan's fear made him very, very angry. "Get out of here you little monsters!" he called out. "Go back to Hell!"

Alan threw the rock. It hit the smallest imp squarely in the back of the head. The imp slowly turned and eyed Alan. Alan remained on his knees, locked in a stare down with the creature in the pouring rain. The other imps stopped their noise and they all turned to look at the three humans lying on the quickly dampening earth.

In a trembling voice, Alan yelled, "I said go back to Hell!"

Father Dingle couldn't endorse such behavior, but he had to admire it.

The imp who'd been hit hunched forward on a gnarled tree branch, looking intensely at Alan. It turned its head to one side, like a dog who's trying to make out whether you have a treat in mind or a trip to the vet, and it made a chuckling noise. The other imps chuckled with it. For a few seconds they chuckled and clucked like overwrought hens. Then with a shake of its head, the small imp flew down and landed in front of Alan who was still kneeling in the mud. Alan gazed down at it. From his vantage point, Father Dingle thought Alan looked like a teacher getting down on his knees to talk to a small and ugly child. The imp turned its head this way and that, clearly thinking. Then it reached out its bony fingers, stroking Alan's chin and his neck, all the while peering into his eyes. It clicked its tongue, still wagging its oversized head from side to side, considering. It rubbed the back of its head where Alan had pelted it with a rock.

Suddenly, it leapt on Alan's neck, biting hard and deep. One bite. It lingered at Alan's neck for a few seconds, tracing the bite mark almost tenderly with its bony claw-like fingernail, then flew back to its companions.

Alan remained on his knees for a few seconds, like a tree after the felling cut. Cowering on the ground, Father Dingle could see the bite mark on Alan's neck. It was a perfect circle of teeth marks...for an instant. Then the blood oozed from the wound, marring its circular perfection, welling up into large beads, dripping down Alan's neck in a stream of crimson. Alan toppled, stiff as a log. He lay unmoving in the mud. The whole swarm of imps gathered and flew off like a dark cloud up through the trees and into the tattered sky.

Alan lay pale and motionless, barely breathing. Father Dingle moved over and took Alan's head in his hand as he tried to keep it from the sodden ground. Alan's blood covered Father Dingle's hand. Father Dingle remained in the graveyard watching Margie's retreating back as she ran through the white tombstones, fiery red hair against her blue sweater. She went to find Sheriff Henry and an ambulance. She was afraid to go back inside for a phone.

Father Dingle did not move as she disappeared into the fog of his rain smeared glasses. He remained kneeling on the ground holding Alan, mud oozing through his pant leg and creeping into his shoes. He did not know whether he held a man or a corpse. He felt that he could not breathe, but his body remained alive. Then realized he was breathing not air but fear. Fear filled his lungs. Fear coursed through his veins. It filled his belly. It slid downwards, and his intestines cramped with it. Every crevice of his body and soul, every crack, every wrinkle, every cavity was full of fear.

The fear that the demons unleashed was a magnet for every other fear he had ever felt, and Father Dingle had always been afraid. This new fear devoured his fear of the dark and expanded. It devoured his fear that he would lose his job. It sucked up his fear of confrontation. His fear of hunger. His fear of sex. His fear of loneliness and his fear of intimacy. As it swallowed up all his other fears, it grew.

Now enormous, the Fear loomed over him. And he recognized it. This was the god he had attempted to pacify all his life. His religion was not an invitation to the sacred and mysterious. His religion was an attempt to keep those things at bay. Hell smashed his illusions with a battering ram...and a message. All his rituals and liturgies, all his attempts to be good had been pointless, because Hell found a way in anyway. He'd been right to be afraid. The universe was and always had been oblivious to his magician's chants and hymns.

This knowledge broke him. For a time, he could no longer summon enough existential vigor to trouble himself. His strength ebbed, and he relaxed himself into the mind of Fear. His soul, drowned in terror, was numb. Submission to Fear had briefly released him from feeling afraid. His God, revealing His true nature, had at last given him the religious ecstasy he had so long been denied. The ecstasy of total detachment.

After the ordeal, Sheriff Henry picked Father Dingle up at the hospital and dropped him at home. Here he was now...in his pajama pants drinking brandy. He'd locked the doors and windows and closed all the drapes. It wasn't until then that the numbness released him. His sense of self-preservation and with it his terror, returned. No one believed them, of course. Alan had been removed to the hospital, still unresponsive. Deputy Smith and Sheriff Henry said they would search for the assailants. Maybe Father Dingle and his staff had been attacked with a pipe bomb they said, searching for a reasonable explanation for the damage and Alan's injury. Father Dingle could see the glances they exchanged when he and Margie told their stories. But Father Dingle knew the explanation. The universe did not have to wait to sneak in through an unlocked window. It did not have a rule book. The universe could simply unleash Hell. And it had, for reasons that were and always would be opaque.

He sat in contemplation of all these things with his cat, Cedric, on his lap. The cat slowly softened Father Dingle's belly with his claws. Father Dingle was a master of ignoring disquiet and apprehension, had been for years. This was different. Fear settled on him like a heavy blanket, pushing against his chest, forcing him to choke down his blackberry brandy through his constricted throat. He felt smothered and had to remind himself to push his breath in and out. He tried praying to the God he'd known before today, but his agitated brain couldn't manage anything more than breathing and drinking, breathing and drinking.

Still, he tried. He tried to think of some reason this had happened. He pondered how. He pondered why. He pondered who. Most of all he pondered whether he was somehow to blame. It was his church after all. He was surely responsible for a portal to Hell in his own church basement. It was at least negligence of some kind. His brain had circled the track until it was exhausted and was now inching back towards the default position. He could make no sense of today's events. Odds were, he wasn't suddenly going to become a brave or useful man. He was finding it hard to repent of his fears. Perhaps fear was the most appropriate response to a universe at its mercy.

After all, what could he do? He had no magic tricks or seminary tidbits to close the portal to Hell. Perhaps it had closed itself. Perhaps it hadn't. No one believed the story, except Margie, and what exactly could a roundish, balding, middle aged priest and twenty-something, part-time church secretary do to fight the powers of Hell? Not one thing he could think of. Not one thing.

In spite of all his efforts, in spite of all his religious supplications to the infinite to leave him alone, the mysterious universe had broken through. This wasn't a good thing – as he had suspected all along. What could he do? He suddenly relaxed back into Infinite Fear. There was nothing he could do. He would simply go back to hoping that the Universal Mystery would leave him alone. What were the odds of such a thing happening again? He would hope the imps had flown away from Whistlestop and far over Knobb Mountain, to some other town, as long as it wasn't his own. Hope that somehow Alan would be okay in the morning. Hope that the church could be put to rights again and that no more portals to Hell would open in the church basement. Hope that he could forget it all and somehow go on. It was a poor tired hope. But it was all he had.

He was exhausted. The brandy was finally doing its work. He stood up. He would get Cedric his tuna, he would go to bed and lock his door and pull up the blankets and he would sleep as long as ever he could. Yes indeed. Certainly, he had a good excuse for calling in sick for a few days. The universe could sort its own damned self out. Father Dingle was done trying to manipulate it. He would hide from it as best he could.

He started to walk to the kitchen when the phone rang. Why hadn't he traded it in for a cell phone as the Bishop suggested? It jangled his nerves. It rang again. That was twice. Another loud, jarring *brrring*. Two more rings and it would stop. Whoever was calling would think he was in bed. Every nerve in his body quivered. The phone itself might have been a small bat winged demon it unnerved him so. It battered his fragile new wall of exhaustion and serene despair.

The final ring shook him into action beyond his control. His hand shot out, quivering and he heard himself answer the phone.

"Hello?" he trembled into the phone.

"Father Dingle! Its Margie," the phone said to him. He removed the phone from his ear and looked at it with distaste.

"Father Dingle, are you there?" she was speaking loudly, and he could still hear her.

He put the phone back to his ear.

"Yes," he said uncertainly.

"What are we going to do? Ellen, my roommate saw one! On her way home, she saw it in the park! They'll have to believe us now Father! We have to..." Margie's voice snapped off as Father Dingle clicked the phone gently back onto the receiver.

"Come, Cedric," he said, his voice quivering. He almost fell over his cat, which was rubbing its face on his leg in anxious anticipation of tuna. But he forced his trembling feet to shuffle toward the kitchen, "It's time for tuna. And then off to bed. If there's one thing I've learned today, Cedric, it's that the only proper response to this universe is fear. And if we swallow enough fear and brandy, we won't feel a thing."

The Laughing Pink Elephant

I didn't come by this story in the usual way. As a rule, most of my Whistlestop stories bubble up from the underground springs of whispered gossip, the main course of church potlucks, and "prayer requests" that are meant more to relay information to the other church goers than to the Lord Almighty. The tales grow up from dinner party conversations that start with "bless her heart" and the little talks at the grocery store when someone asks, "did you hear about?" They start with a shake of the head by the all-knowing bar maids at the Pop-A-Top on the wrong side of town, or from Emma Washington, the seemingly telepathic former third grade teacher who somehow knows someone who knows someone who knows something about everyone. In this case though, I got the story right from the proverbial horse's mouth. Or actually, from a friend of mine, a history professor named Mark. Mark called me up one stormy summer evening demanding to see me. He wanted to discuss an "incident."

"An incident?" I asked. I was busy, deep in the middle of writing a story that had just started to move in the right direction. I didn't need the distraction.

"An incident that occurred in Whistlestop," he spat out the name of the town like a bad taste. "I have to talk about it. To someone." His voice was intense. He spoke quickly, "Somebody told me you had relatives up there."

"What were you doing in Whistlestop?" I asked. Whistlestop is not exactly on most people's must-see list, "And I have a summer house up there I inherited from my Aunt Nancy. Why?"

"It's all part of the story," he said testily.

There was silence for a moment as the thunder splintered the air and the rain pelted the wavy panes of my office windows. I was intrigued but uneasy. The storm lashed the outside of my window like the furies torturing the damned.

"Sure," I said. "I guess. You want to come over here?"

"I can't," he said. "I have a night class. You're going to have to come my way."

"Ummm...," I looked out at the pounding rain.

"Seriously," he said. "I need you to hear this." Had his voice cracked a little?

I sighed. "How about the coffee shop by your office?"

"How about the bar on Fourth?" he said. "I'm going to need a drink."

Mark was a reasonable person and a good teacher. I couldn't imagine him drinking before class. After all, he taught history not English. Now I was interested. Seriously interested. Maybe I could get to the car without drowning or being torn asunder by a lightning bolt.

"I'll be there when I get there," I said. "In case you haven't noticed, there's a monsoon going on out there."

"Ha!" he shouted into the phone. "Compared to what I've just been through? A monsoon is child's play. Just meet me at four." He hung up abruptly.

I met Mark at the bar. He already had a table and a whiskey. One storm had melted into another and my hair was plastered to my forehead in spite of my umbrella. I sloshed my way to a booth in the back and slid across a cracked leather seat opposite Mark.

"Really?" I asked, as I sat down. "You don't drink whiskey."

"I do now," he took a long swallow and coughed and sputtered out the word, "Whistlestop." He shook his head. He took another swallow and I noticed his eyes looked a little wild.

"How many does that make?" I said, indicating the whiskey.

He shrugged, "Just two...so far. I'll probably need more."

"I'll drive you back to campus," I said. Should be a happening class tonight, I thought.

"I'll walk," he looked absently into his whiskey.

I pointed toward the furious storm outside. He shrugged again. We sat in the strange noisy silence fashioned of other people's conversations, the clinking of glasses, and the clamor of the storm outside while he struggled through a few sips of his drink. You have to be patient with Mark. He can't or won't just spit anything out no matter how you press him. So, I ordered a beer and peered out through the slithering liquid, watching trees wave desperately in the parking lot until I heard him clear his throat.

He finally leaned back in his chair and began, "It...it was such an ordinary day. I was just going over to Asheville to read a paper, you know?"

I nodded. "And..."

"And...Jerry convinced me to take the scenic route up the mountain. Said there was this little town up at the top on the Tennessee side I could probably make by lunch time."

"Whistlestop," I said.

"Yeah," he said. "Whistlestop."

"Go on," I said.

"Well, the first thing I see, as I'm coming into town is this big, freaking, pink Victorian House with a weird sign out front. An elephant in a bathtub."

"The Laughing Pink Elephant," I said.

It's an antique/junk/oddities store located in a sprawling pink and yellow Victorian at the western edge of town, just a block or two from the town square. He noticed it, as everyone does, largely because of the gigantic, aging wooden sign displaying a large pink elephant sitting in a claw foot tub and holding what appears to be a champagne glass.

Most people feel the expression on its face is more pensive than hilarious, but the owners of the place quite stubbornly cling to the idea that the elephant is laughing. The sign has been a target of the town beautification committee - whose members have refused to weigh in on the emotional condition of the elephant but have focused more on the fact that the sign doesn't appropriately represent the aesthetics of the town as a whole. Or as Mary Edelson Brooks, the head of the Whistlestop Beautification Committee, once told me, it's just plain tacky. Harold and Angel Wright are the owners and they'll never change it. Harold's dad, who considered himself something of an artist, painted it.

"Anyway," Mark said, "I woke up that morning and it was like, the perfect summer day, you know? And I thought to myself, why not follow Jerry's lunatic plan? Of course, I was pretty frazzled by the time I got there. I ended up behind a tractor going five miles an hour for fifteen miles, and, of course, the air conditioner broke."

I nodded, "Lots of farm equipment on the roads up that way."

"Plus, when I opened the windows, I started sneezing," he looked morosely out into the pouring rain, "I thought it was such a pretty little town."

I knew what he meant. As you come through the last of the hairpin turns up the mountain road and into

Whistlestop, you see huge leafy trees spreading their arms above the shrubs, flowering trees, and roses. A few small white cottages are scattered on the side of the road and then bigger and more beautiful houses, some of them even from the antebellum period. The Civil War never quite made it up to Whistlestop, other than a few raiding parties.

"I mean there were flower petals wafting in the breeze," he said, "I guess it kind of lulled me into a false sense of security."

"Whistlestop does that to people," I said. "The first time I went there..."

"Don't interrupt," he frowned. "This is hard enough."

I clammed up and watched him swirl some whiskey around on the table with his finger for a minute while I waited for him to continue. He finally looked up and began again.

Mark told me that as he drove past The Laughing Pink Elephant, it occurred to him that he had forgotten to pick up a birthday gift for his mother. He thought he might stop, find a restroom, buy a gift and inquire as to the best place for lunch. He made his way through the parking lot, taking a moment (as most people do) to contemplate the emotionally ambiguous animal on the sign and decided that the elephant - which he thought was more of a salmon color than a true pink - appeared to be somewhat drunk but did not seem to be laughing about it.

When he got out of the car, he realized finding a restroom had become somewhat more mission critical than his other goals. So, he walked into the foyer and politely asked the old hippie lady with big gray hair and glasses for directions. The woman in question was Angel, not a hippie at all. She'd attended a Church of God when she was a child and had it pounded in her head that God preferred women with long hair. However, she had no time for the elaborate buns or beehives of her foremothers, so she pulled her long, gray hair into a ponytail, hoping that would placate the Almighty.

Mark noted that Angel was looking at the account book and barely seemed to notice him. She just muttered the word "left" and pointed vaguely toward the hallway that opened perpendicular to the foyer.

As he walked away, Mark heard her say, "Make sure it's that door in the little room before you get to the antique meat grinder, not the room after. That's a closet." Mark was mystified but thought he could probably figure it out as he went.

He figured it would have a sign with one of those annoying little proverbs about sprinkling and tinkling or maybe an elephant with its legs crossed looking desperate or something. At this juncture in his story, his pressing need to have me understand the details of his quest for a toilet was not clear.

Mark passed several rooms on the side until he came to an antique machine with a turn handle that looked as though it must be a grinder of some sort, so he brought himself up short and turned into the room just before it. The room was packed with oddities. He saw an old gnome sitting on a brass elephant planter, some eyeless wooden masks and an old ventriloquist's dummy hanging from the walls, a few shelves with ancient and rusted metal objects and some old tin advertising signs. There was a stuffed raccoon with its tail broken so that it stuck out at a right angle halfway up. He apparently needed to stop for a moment to linger on the details before he could bring himself to relate the dark heart of his story – whatever that was.

He paused at the memory of the room, which he supposed was a store room and shuddered. His story stopped momentarily until I ordered him another whiskey. He continued after he'd taken a sip.

He remembered that the only light in the room came from one large open window with an ancient, torn screen through which a small stream of flies was buzzing. In the back of the room to the left, there was a large Moose head with one antler at a slight list, under it there was a door. It was unmarked.

"The moose had a strange smell," Mark said. His hands trembled as he brought the whiskey to his lips. "I should have known. I just...it felt like fate. In spite of the smell, I walked to the door. Then again, it seemed silly not to just open the door and go in."

I leaned forward and patted his hand. I used my napkin to quietly soak up the amber liquid that threatened the cuff of his dress shirt.

He pushed past the strange smell and feeling of dread, reached out and pulled on the door handle. A broom fell out and hit him on the head, before the door opened more than a few inches.

"Crap, it's the closet," he said to himself.

He caught the broom and attempted to simply stuff it back into the tightly packed closet, but in the next second, he could feel the entire contents of the closet pressing heavily on the door. A mop flopped out of the gap and the broom fell back out after it. He braced the door with his left shoulder, pushing in the mop and broom with his right hand. Something heavy fell against the door and he reached in further to push it back into place too. He tried to shut the door on the avalanche. He heard the pinging and rattling of small things falling onto the closet floor. He started to sweat a little. He didn't want anyone to catch him opening the closet door. Would they think he was stealing? Prying? If nothing else, it would be terribly loud and embarrassing if the contents of the closet came clanging out at his feet.

Still pressing the door with his left shoulder, he opened it a little further, so he could reach in and push the mess into place, close the door and quietly leave the room. He would just have to find the restroom on his own. He craned his head around the edge of the door into the darkness and quickly pushed his right hand through the opening to hold back the wave of junk. The dusty light trickled through the air and flies buzzing over his shoulder and fell on the objects inside.

He peered in to see what he was up against, and just under the heel of his hand he could see an oval of dewy, velvety white. On either side of his hand was a dark black marble-like sphere. He couldn't make out exactly what it was in the dim light of the closet. When he thought about it later, he also said that his brain probably didn't want to know.

The shapes resolved themselves slowly, he said, by degrees. They resolved into a face. It was a heart shaped face, pale, pointed and most absolutely...dead. Cold and dead. It was a dead woman. A corpse.

"I knew once I could process...you know...that I could see it was a woman...I knew she was dead. Of course...you feel it...I can't say what it feels like. But you feel it all the way through." He shivered and stared into space.

I gave an involuntary start. He took another sip.

"So, I'm holding up this body with my hand and do you know what starts going through my head?" he stared at me, then gave a dry laugh. "Dead as a doornail. I mean the phrase 'dead as a doornail.' It just ran through my mind in a circle. Doornail? Doornail? Why doornail?" He laughed a hard laugh again. "My brain just shut the hell down."

Whistlestop, I thought. You have outdone yourself this time.

Mark spent some amount of time searching his mental file cabinet for the provenance of the phrase. He couldn't say how long he pondered why doornails had come to represent death. Then with a clang, the mental file slammed shut. His brain turned its attention back to the shocking fact that he was propping up a corpse with his hand. His brain wanted to know what he intended to do about it. He thought about this question. He wanted to pull back his hand but was unable to make his body do anything. He gazed into the glassy eyes. They gazed back, serene. The corpse was pinned against the mountain of junk in the closet by his hand. The moment settled uncomfortably into eternity. Not moving meant he was in contact with a dead body. Moving meant that it would fall forward, and any animation seemed worse than the stillness. He asked his brain if it had an answer for that. It did not. He said he was wondering if there was a resolution or whether he himself might stay there until he was also a corpse, when a fly settled on his thumb. With a start, he jerked his hand backwards. The corpse toppled forward, caught in an avalanche of ancient cleaning supplies and oddities.

The sudden landslide flung itself on him and the whole mess hit him square on the chest. His feet, spinning in place in a pointless attempt at escape, slid out from under him. The thick solid weight fell on his chest while various wooden handles bonked him in the head.

He said he thought he screamed but didn't feel any sound coming out. He pushed out from under the body and scrambled up and against the wall. Then he looked down. The brief skirmish had rolled the corpse onto her back. He could see that her yellow and blue flowered dress was stuck to her belly in a thick, dark mass that widened into a large stain, swallowing the tiny blue flowers like the night coming on. One flat black shoe still clung to her right foot. He wondered if someone had taken the time to put it back on. The other foot was bare. He could see that her toes had been painted in bright pink nail polish. The brown eyes stared ahead pointlessly. Wavy brown hair lay in tangled streamers around several mops and brooms. The head rested on a feather duster which flirtatiously stuck out from behind a bruised and bloody ear.

Mark shook his head and swallowed a lot of whiskey at once. "She looked like a show girl for the damned," he said.

I said nothing. I wasn't sure what to say.

"At first, I just looked at her. I thought about it all rather calmly. There was blood on her hands. I thought that she must have tried to press the wound or fought with her killer as she was dying," he bent his head over his drink. "I thought someone must have cleaned her up a little and put shoes on her before moving her there. They couldn't have killed her there. There would have been blood everywhere. I could see...at least I thought I saw...that her stomach was slashed nearly open. It was hard to tell because some old towels had fallen on her. And then I thought she must not have been dead very long or she would smell even worse. And I wondered why? Why would someone put her in the janitor's closet?"

He took his head out of his hands, shook himself out of the memory and continued. He said he had finally realized that he had to quit thinking and do something. The contents of hell and a janitor's closet had burst forth on top of him and his mind rooted for some appropriate reaction. The right thing to do.

He wanted to walk calmly out to the foyer and alert someone. He would have to step over the corpse to do it. His body failed him as some primitive awe for the dead overtook him. He decided then that he could at least call to someone. He opened his mouth and was surprised to hear an eerie and trembling sound force its way out of the depths of his body. There seemed to be nothing more he could do.

Shortly after that, he saw some people come running into the room and stop short on the other side of the corpse in the pile of junk. The gray haired hippie woman, Angel, a guy with a beard and big glasses he later discovered was Harold Wright, the owner, and a guy with wavy black and gray hair in a plaid shirt named Dan. From the description, I was pretty sure he was describing Dan Cunningham, owner of Whistlestop's Used Car Emporium. Dan's always running around town, nobody could ever figure out how he kept the place open.

Mark was nearly insensible, panting and moaning and holding a dust mop between himself and the corpse as though he was trying to ward it off. When he saw the other human beings enter the room, he leapt toward the comforting sight of the living, jumping nimbly over the body and landing with his left foot in the mop bucket. He slid gracelessly across the room and bounced off the far wall and fell flat on his back. His head hit the floor with a solid thunk.

The three of them, Harold, Angel and Dan, stood over him for a minute, Mark said, staring. Then Harold helped him up and plopped him on a stool in the corner.

He said Harold stared at him for a minute and looked at the pile of junk and said, "I thought I heard a commotion in here."

Angel said, "I thought it was you, Harold. Dropping things again."

Mark was uncertain for a moment if any of them even knew there was a body in all the junk that had fallen from the closet. He shakily pointed it out.

"Damn...sure enough. It's a dead woman," Dan said. He walked over and looked at the body.

"Get back!" Harold said, "You're not supposed to move the body."

"No cussing in my store," Angel told Dan.

Then the three of them helped Mark out of the room and someone, Mark didn't remember who, called the Sheriff.

"So, we're all in the lobby right?" said Mark, "And Dan turns and looks at me and says, 'Why in the Hell would you come in here opening doors like that? What on God's green earth were you thinking, son?'"

"I bet Angel didn't like that," I said. "After she told Dan to quit cussing."

Mark glared at me. "How did you...?" he said. Then he sighed, "Yeah. She told him that she had already said she didn't want to hear any cussing. Because, you know if there's one thing that can make a murder worse than it already is, it would be saying a swear word."

He went on, "So then they all look at me and Angel says, 'Didn't you say you had to use the restroom? That's the broom closet. Why were you opening up the broom closet?'

He paused dramatically, "Do you get it? They were upset because I had opened the door. Not that there was a corpse in the closet. There was a dead woman. And they wanted to know why I had opened the door." I sincerely wished I could express more surprise.

"So, what happened next?" I asked. "Did they call Sheriff Henry?"

"So first," Mark said, "That Dan guy makes a joke that maybe I opened the closet because I wanted to help sweep up. Then...uh...Harold...he starts asking me how I got lost trying to find the bathroom. He was like 'didn't Angel tell you it was in the room right before the antique meat grinder'? And I said yes. I saw it right out in the hall, the meat grinder I mean. He's asking me about a meat grinder. And I'm explaining how I got lost going to find a toilet. And all the while she's still dead. Just lying there. And I'm talking about not being able to find my way to the toilet."

He took a rather large swig of his whiskey. He paused dramatically. "So, guess what?"

He waited for me to respond, frowning.

"Um what?" I played along.

He ran his fingers through his hair and then he suddenly giggled. I resolved to have the bartender cut him off.

"What I saw was a coffee grinder. It wasn't a meat grinder at all." He laughed helplessly. "They sold the meat grinder the day before. Angel forgot. Her directions were wrong."

"I bet Harold explained the difference to you," I said.

Mark nodded. "At length. He said he didn't want me to get confused and get into this kind of a situation again." Mark giggled, and a slight hiccup bubbled up and caught him by surprise. "A situation. With a corpse. Because I didn't know the difference between a coffee grinder and a meat grinder." He swallowed the last of his alcohol at once.

Then he frowned, "You don't think I will, do you?" he asked. "Get into another situation like this one?"

"I'm pretty sure that's not the sort of thing that happens twice," I said, trying to comfort him. "Especially if you stay out of Whistlestop."

"I can promise you that!" he said, thumping his fist on the table.

"So…?" I asked, gently reaching across the table and moving his arms out of danger of the spilled liquid. "What happened?"

Mark said someone must have finally called the sheriff. At the same time, the "situation" at The Laughing Pink Elephant somehow telegraphed itself through the clairvoyant atmosphere that envelops every small town. So, by the time the police showed up there was already a crowd out front. Sheriff Henry left Mark with Officer Watson to give his statement, then he was seated on an uncomfortable wooden bench in the front of the store, an old church pew he thought. He wondered how anyone sat in the dreadful thing for any length of time, much less with someone droning on about sky fairies and whatnot.

No one told him whether or not he was free to go. The Deputy was out front fending people off. Mark could see Dan talking to Officer Watson quietly, occasionally pointing at Mark and shaking his head. He heard a snatch of their conversation. It turned out the corpse was the wife of a janitor who'd worked there before. Their conversation turned back to Mark at some point.

"Well, I've never seen him around here and why he in that closet was?" Dan was saying.

Angel was sitting on a stool behind the counter bemoaning the fact *a woman had been killed in her store* and threatening to faint every few minutes. Harold had grabbed an old feathered fan from one of the antique booths and he was fanning Angel and saying, "Now, now! I'm sure it wasn't personal. Just convenient. Could have been anyone's closet."

Mark noted the feathers on Harold's fan were huge and ugly. Maybe turkey feathers he thought.

Then Angel took to sniffling and saying, "Lord everybody in town told Sarah Lawson, I told her, her mama told her, not to marry that boy. Sweet Jesus, that boy never was a lick of good."

Harold patted her absently on the shoulder, occasionally stopping to wipe his forehead with a handkerchief.

"I could still smell the body," said Mark. "I don't know if it was my imagination or if the smell had soaked into my clothes. I just needed to get out of there." He shivered and wrinkled his nose. "I think I can still smell it. Sometimes I still smell it. Took four showers when I got home. I still smell it." He inspected his empty glass and looked at me. I sighed and ordered him another.

"So," Mark said, "I'm just sitting. Listening, you know. Angel complaining because maybe they have to close the store. Someone has to clean up the mess and, of course, that someone is going to be her, then she's crying and says, 'poor Sarah,' talking about how stupid the dead girl was to have married her husband. Why did her mom let her get a job at the Pop-A-Top? No decent girl would work there. Harold is trying to explain the difference between a coffee grinder and a meat grinder to Officer Watson..."

He shrugs, "By this time there are some other people who've somehow wormed their way inside. Some woman is quietly asking Harold what he thinks it's going to do to tourism. Tourism for God's sakes!"

"They finally let in a tall awkward looking-priest, from St. Bartholomew's or Barnabus. Or something. A substitute because the old one went bonkers," he said, "And he pats my arm and stammers out something about helping me and can he pray with me. And I say 'Umm...no thanks' Then he patters off to 'help' some of the other people."

"And Dan keeps saying, 'It's a Hell of a thing' and Angel is interrupting herself to tell him not to cuss and one of the officers is on the phone to his wife telling her that he's going to be late to dinner and that he can't help it she has popovers..." He trailed off and stared into space.

"Then," he said, "I hear a commotion outside. Officer Watson says that the hearse that's going to take her to the coroner's office has a flat. Poor, poor Sarah. She was murdered...and then there's just this... clown show."

I could tell he was drifting away. The whiskey was getting to him.

"So, what did you do?" I asked.

"At that point," Mark yawned, "I realized that the dead woman was probably the most sensible person in town, even if it was damned hard to get over the way she smelled. So, I get up and go out and stand by the hearse. They've left her there on a stretcher in a body bag on her own. Everyone else is off, I don't know, trying to call triple A or something. The Sheriff and the Deputy come out, get in their car and drive away."

"I'm standing there alone with the body and I say, 'I'm sorry. I'm really, really sorry you're dead and I'm sorry you had to live in this awful town.'"

I didn't know what to say to that.

Mark tried to explain. "I wasn't being flippant. I just didn't know what else to say to her. It seemed like someone owed her an apology. I mean, the murderer sure, but an apology for all of them...us."

He sighed. "Then I felt my keys in my pocket. I could see my car across the parking lot. I just got in it and left. Came home. Took about six showers. Now it's today and I'm totally drunk. Here we all are."

We sat quietly for a moment. Then Mark said, "So do you think they'll come after me or something? Nobody told me I was free to go or anything."

I thought about it for a minute. "No," I said. They've probably already forgotten you. You'll just end up being some stranger in town in one of the stories they tell themselves."

He nodded. "Good," he said.

I called the school and cancelled class and took him home and left him on his couch. As far as I know, no one from Whistlestop ever contacted him about the case and he never went back.

The dead woman in the closet is another story, worth telling but not today.

The Strange Disappearance of Edna Brown

Edna Louise Brown disappeared clean out of Whistlestop. The town didn't even realize that Edna had disappeared until she didn't show up to choir practice one Wednesday night. Edna worked as manager of The Dollar Store. She lived in a small, white, two-bedroom house she'd inherited from her father. She wasn't beautiful. She wasn't rich. She wasn't and had never been married. Her son was Homeless Tom. She'd raised him quietly on her own, never naming the father. She'd gone back to church after a while, joined the choir, but she'd never become a member or even thought about joining the Home Circle. Even God's forgiveness had its limits.

When Sheriff Henry arrived, the first thing he noticed was how normal everything looked. The tiny white house, with its disproportionately large porch, stood calmly on the fresh cut grass. With one set of curtains drawn it appeared to be winking at him as he crunched down the long gravel drive. He could see the clothes fluttering on the line in the side yard. Her plain old box of a car sat serenely in the drive.

Upon inspection, Sheriff Henry found that the double pink azaleas with the white centers at the edge of the drive, the ones she was so proud of, had been crushed and broken. Tire tracks in the dust led to the shrubs. He walked onto the porch and found a blue enamelware cup. One window had been left open. He went into the kitchen and found three dead flies stuck in the sludge of dried tea leaves in a china cup. The door was unlocked. There was a tea towel wadded on the counter. A few unwashed dishes looked out of place. There was no sign of violence and no sign of Edna.

The only strange thing that the Sheriff saw was a large black cat, or so he thought, running through the cane down by the creek out back of the house. There was not a sign of another human anywhere around the place.

Three full days before the town of Whistlestop knew that Edna was missing, two strangers were standing alongside a black car parked on the gravel turn-around right outside of town, next to Fish Kill creek, a waterway that had run toxic blue, red and yellow during the mill years. Now it was full of fish again, though it still had more than its share of two headed catfish or strangely mutated minnows with bubble eyes and lumpy backs. The two men weren't thinking of the mutated fish. They had other things to think about that day.

The car they were standing next to might have felt quite at home next to a two-headed fish. It was big and round and bulging, shiny black with chrome fins coming off it at odd angles. The two men had immaculate gray summer suits and hats. They were handsome men. One of the men had a bright red tie, one had a blue. The man with the red tie was a little taller and heavier than the other. Otherwise, they could have been twins. Brothers for sure. Both had the same long nose, high cheekbones, slender necks and broad shoulders. The suits fit beautifully but both men shifted and tugged at sleeves and shirt necks, pulled and loosened their ties, like grade school boys at Easter. Blue tie looked particularly uncomfortable, and tired.

He coughed for a moment, placing his hand on his side. He put his hands on his hips and rolled his shoulders back.

"I can't get comfortable this time," he said.

"Well you look snappy anyway," said Red Tie, adjusting the lapels on Blue Tie's suit jacket, "It won't be long now. Won't be long."

"I won't make it much longer before I go nuts," the other man agreed.

"Maybe she'll be glad to have things over with too. I expect she's just tired by now. You know how time works around here," said Red Tie, "Drags on if you ask me."

"Maybe. I don't know, Carl," Blue Tie said.

He turned and walked a few steps towards the creek bed. He stopped before he got too close and stuck out his tongue. He touched it with his finger. He darted his tongue in and out and slid it against his teeth. "My tongue feels thick. This always happens. Feels like ith's in my way." He turned and spat on the dirt.

"Dang it, Larry," Carl was beginning to do the same thing with his own tongue. "Blah. Can't talk..." he trailed off and slid his tongue around until he bit it. He spat out blood.

"Ouch!" Carl said. "Geez Larry, you cannot think about these things that hard. Remember?"

"Sorry," Larry said. "I'll do my best. I can't quite get connected this time. That's the problem. I can't get it..." He bent over and took a few deep breaths and coughed, "Can't get it together."

"It's okay," Carl said. "I know you're not yourself. Maybe shake it out a little."

He grabbed Larry by the shoulders and tumbled him gently about for a moment.

"Get ahold of yourself, settle in, even if only for a little while. It's me that will be stuck here. Lord knows, I should be the one nervous. This time around looks like it's going to be rough. Now settle in," Carl said.

Larry readjusted his jacket and patted Carl's shoulder. "Sure enough, Carl. Sure enough. That feels more like it."

Carl glanced at his watch, "We need to leave here in five minutes."

Larry started fidgeting with his ear.

Carl leaned forward and peered at the ear, frowning. He twisted it. Larry winced.

"Geez," said Carl as he stood back for another look, "Better. It'll do for no longer than it has to. Have a smoke?"

Carl took out a cigarette and offered one to Larry. They stood propped against the car watching the thin smoke drift towards the creek.

"How far to Edna's house?" Larry asked.

"Only a few miles," Carl responded, he checked his watch again. He watched the creek bubbling past as he blew smoke into the warm summery air and then traced patterns in it with his finger. He glanced at his watch again.

He threw the cigarette on the ground and stubbed it out with his toe.

"It's time," he said.

"I suppose so," Larry said. He threw his cigarette down too.

"Larry?" Carl said.

"Yes?" Larry answered.

"I'm going to miss you buddy."

Carl got into the driver's seat. He flung the car into gear and tore onto the road.

"Lordy, this thing is hard to drive, Larry," Carl said, wrestling the wheel around with one arm, "Should have gotten a newer one maybe."

"Nah," said Larry. "The new ones are ugly. Have you seen them?"

Both men were silent for a moment as the car bolted forward. Carl kept it at a steady speed in spite of potholes, rocks and cattle grates in his way.

"Take it easy Carl. Wanna get this thing there in one piece if we can. Remember last time," Larry's voice bounced and wobbled, and his teeth clattered together as Carl bounced them down the road.

Carl checked his watch, which he'd put on his right arm, and the car wobbled towards the opposite ditch.

Every curve and every straightaway met the huge car at the same breakneck speed. Larry slid back and forth in the front seat, slamming into the passenger door and then nearly flying through the windshield without a murmur. Carl kept himself somewhat stationary by hooking one arm out the open window and driving with his other. Occasionally he let go of the wheel and checked his watch, catching the car each time before it left the road for a ditch.

The monstrous black car finally hurtled onto a little lane with a farmhouse in the distance. Before long, Carl slammed down the dirt driveway at top speed, and the car slid into the grass, barely missing another car and flattening a stand of azaleas. Carl walked around to the passenger side and opened the door. Larry spilled onto the lawn.

Carl picked Larry up and straightened him out. He shook him again slightly.

"Good luck," he said. He backed up and squinted at Larry, inspecting him. "Not bad."

He checked his watch, "Just hang in there. Remember, you don't have long, Cinderella!"

Carl tipped his hat, got in the enormous black car, and left.

Larry turned to the porch and began to walk up the stairs, slowly, nervously rolling his hat in his hands. Before he reached the second step, a tall, broad woman flew out of the door and dashed to the edge of the stairs. Larry stumbled back and caught himself with a railing.

"My azaleas! Come back here!" The woman yelled at the retreating car. She shook her fist.

Then she looked down the stairs and noticed Larry, "Was that your friend who ran over my azaleas?" she asked, arms crossed over her chest, "Who are you and what do you want?"

Larry stood still, staring at her, "Edna, it's…"

She pushed up her glasses and pointed a finger at him, "I don't need anything. I don't want anything. I'm not buying anything, and that includes Jesus or any other deity you may be representing, so you can trot on down the road and find your friend. You can tell him he owes me some azaleas."

Larry took a deep breath and looked up at her, "Edna?" he said, "It's me!"

The woman stared. She squinted and then moved her head up and down, so she could see him through different parts of her bifocal glasses, "Larry?"

"Yes Edna," he said, "I'm back."

Her hands made fists, fingers curling into themselves. She stood contemplating him, eyebrows knotted together thinking. A muscle in her jaw worked. She pursed her lips and put her chin up – looking way up at some wispy clouds in the bright blue sky. Collecting herself. She finally sighed. She put her hands on her hips, turned back to him.

Larry put his hand on the rail and ratcheted himself up straight, so she could see him. He took a deep breath and made a small sharp sound. He put his hand on his side for a second.

"Are you sick?" she asked, finally. The question sounded softer than she wanted it to.

Larry thought about the question, "Guess you could say so." He shrugged it off.

Edna didn't say anything more for a moment. She stared over his head at the flattened pink flower bush in the yard.

"After all these years," she said, apparently to the azaleas, "If it isn't Larry. Good God Almighty."

Larry didn't say anything.

"Lord help, if the first thing you did wasn't to flatten my grandmother's azaleas," she still spoke over him rather than to him. She didn't move out of his way or ask him in.

"Sorry," Larry said, "Carl was driving."

"Humph. Carl," Edna snorted, "Your brother never could drive. I'd have thought he would have had time to practice, as long as it's been since you two came through town."

"Edna," Larry said, "Could I have a glass of water?"

Edna brushed back the graying hair that was falling into her face and sighed, "Who says I'm going to let you in?"

Larry took off his hat, "I don't have to come in Edna. I can sit right there on the porch." He pointed at the white porch swing with its cheerful blue gingham pillows.

"Fine," Edna said, "Sit on the porch."

She stumped off and the screen door slammed behind her. When she came out with water, Larry had deposited himself in the porch swing. She handed him a blue enamelware mug.

"Thanks," Larry said. The swing squeaked back and forth for a minute. Squee, squee, squee. They could hear the sound of a truck out on the main road. Bees buzzed. A slight breeze rustled the leaves. The too sweet smell of privet drifted from back by the creek. Edna stood looking at him over the top of her glasses. Larry tipped the cup up and swallowed about half the water at once, nearly choking himself.

"Well. I'm waiting," Edna said finally, "Why are you here?"

"I told you I would be back," Larry said. "Here I am."

"Ha!" Edna said, "I expected you somewhat sooner."

"I came back as soon as I could Edna," Larry said. He glanced at his watch, "And just in time too."

"This was as soon as you could? This is right on time?" Edna asked, "Thirty years? You told me you traveled. Thirty years you traveled?"

Edna folded her arms across her chest, "What am I supposed to do with this now? We have a son, Larry. His name is Tom. Did you know that? Why would you show up now? What good is that to anybody, I'd like to know?"

Larry squeaked the rocker back and forth, "I came back as soon as I could come back. I had to come back. I know about Tom. That's one of the reasons Carl came back with me. He's going to help take care of Tom. He's Tom's, errr...uncle? That's right isn't it?"

Edna plopped down in a rocking chair. She faced Larry. "Oh my God," she said, "That's what you're going to go with? After thirty years. That you knew we had a son and thirty years was the soonest you could make it back?"

Larry nodded, "It's true," he said. He coughed for a few seconds and then hit himself in the chest. He slugged down the rest of the water and licked his lips. He was sweating.

Edna sat shaking her head for a few minutes. She couldn't take in that much tomfoolery at one time.

"This is pretty weird," Edna said, at last, "To be honest, I don't know what to say. I told Tom you were dead." Edna sat for a few minutes rocking, "Of all things..." she said more to herself than Larry.

Larry was staring at her. He was smiling at her and rolling his hat in his hands. "You're still a beautiful woman Edna."

Edna frowned at him over her glasses. She sighed, "I was never a beautiful woman, Larry. That's why I was such an easy mark. I'm a large woman with a flat nose and hands like hams and a man's feet. My mistake was letting you convince me for those few days that I was beautiful. So, don't simper at me now."

"You were beautiful," he said. He paused and breathed in and out a few times. He hit himself on the chest and gave a rumbling cough. "Beautiful...to me."

"Maybe that was your mistake," she said. They said nothing for a moment. She almost caught a memory, the memory of feeling beautiful, but it slipped past, leaving her strangely bereft.

The squee, squee, squee of the swing stopped and Larry made a choking noise. He hit his chest again and caught his breath. He smiled at Edna.

Edna wiped her glasses on her stained cotton skirt and then peered at Larry, "Are you alright Larry?"

"No," said Larry. Then he made a strange burbling noise. "I'm not alright Edna. That's why I'm having a hard time explaining things. Can we go for a walk?"

"You don't appear to be any shape for walking," Edna said, "and besides, I'm not sure why I should. I'm not really sure why I'm even sitting here talking to you at all if I'm honest. Curiosity more than anything I guess."

"I don't want to go far," Larry said. He rose from the swing holding his side. He wheezed a little and swallowed hard, then seemed to regain himself.

"Come with me Edna," he said, "Please?"

"I think this is how the trouble started the first time," Edna replied. She sighed, "Curiosity killed the cat and following a boy into the woods got me pregnant."

"Please Edna," Larry said, "I want to explain something important to you. It affects you as much as me," he coughed and wiped his lips on his handkerchief, "I thought you might have understood, but I can see you don't."

"I don't understand why you can't tell me right here on the porch," she said.

"I want to walk up the hill with you one more time Edna," he said, "I won't be here in this spot again, I think. Not like this."

He touched her hand with his. She slipped right back through time to that one moment when she felt beautiful. Edna closed her eyes. She remembered the touch of Larry's hand on her leg. She remembered the scent of his hair oil. Her daddy had almost convinced himself some boy had forced himself on her. That wasn't true. She'd never done anything so willingly in her life. No amount of church had so much as made her regret a minute of that night, the night when she finally gave in, hard as she'd tried. She wished things had turned out different, sure, but that night was still hers.

She opened her eyes and came back to the present. Larry was not the strange beautiful boy that she remembered. He was still handsome, but he looked tired and sick. She felt more pity than anger she supposed. She certainly wasn't afraid of him.

Still it surprised her that she found herself saying, "Let's go then. If you need to get this off your chest, let's get it done. An apology won't hurt my feelings. Then we'll find Carl and he can do what he likes with you. But leave Tom out of this. He hasn't laid eyes on you for this thirty years. No reason to drag him into things now. I told him you were dead."

"I will be something like that soon enough," Larry said, "Soon enough."

Edna put one sturdy arm around Larry and helped him down the porch stairs.

"The last thing I need is you to die right here and now," she told him, "I think you've caused your share of trouble. So how about you stay alive until you've said your piece."

They walked into the side yard, and slowly into the woods behind her house taking the path up the hill, stopping every few minutes for Larry to put his hand on his side and catch his breath. The breath he caught now had a metallic rasp to it. Edna had never heard such before. He'd been a smoker. She guessed that was the problem. Helping him walk up the hill somehow made her feel better. She was the healthy one, the one that had made it. She could afford him a little sympathy.

"I never thought about you coming back again," Edna said, "Not after the first year or two. If I had thought about you coming back, I would have expected I would be madder at you. As it is, I guess I haven't thought about you enough to get angry. I was busy." This was only a little bit true. Larry had appeared in Edna's dreams and fantasies often enough, but Edna felt her pride demanded the fabrication.

Larry just nodded. He was leading her up the path toward the clearing by the blackberry thicket, where their brief love affair had taken place.

When they finally reached the clearing, Larry sat on a log. Edna sat next to him. The moss felt cool and spongy underneath her. The leaf mold smelled like time, decaying slowly. She was, she found, anxious to hear his story. It would be an excuse certainly, probably a lie, but she hoped it would be a good one. Life certainly hadn't gotten any more interesting since he left. Hard yes. Complicated certainly. But that wasn't the same as interesting. Larry had been the one remarkable thing that had happened to her. Larry and Tom.

For a few moments he was unable to speak. Enda let him catch his breath while she breathed in the smell of moss and leaves. She felt a small cool draft of air dry the sweat on her forehead. This part of the forest seemed home to strange memories of a different timeline, one where Larry had coached their son Tom's baseball team, one where she had stayed home and baked and worn aprons and been the kind of mom Tom needed her to be. Maybe he would have turned out a little differently. A timeline where she had a lover to come home to everyday, where someone made her feel wanted, a lifetime of devotion instead of one night of passion. Memories of things that hadn't happened flitted around her head. She felt she could almost reach out and catch one if she tried.

"You know Tom's not quite right? Not stupid, just different," she said, "He's a wanderer like you. Maybe it would have been different if you'd come back."

"I am back Edna," he said. "Carl will watch out for Tom. Because we have to go away. Together. Me and you Edna."

"Larry," she answered him, scooting away a little. "I came here with you because you said you were going to explain some things. I think I deserve an explanation of why you left. What I don't deserve after all this time is for you to hit me up with some crazy plan to run away together after I've done all the hard work of raising our child. It's not as if we are still lovers. I have a life. It doesn't include you."

She pointed her finger at him, "But I'm not leaving until I hear your explanation. Lie or truth – just make it good."

Larry stared at her. Straight into her eyes without looking left or right, "I told you I had to travel. This was the soonest point in the stream where I could find you again."

"And?" Edna said. She realized she had secretly expected him to come up with a romantic and magnificent excuse, one that would make everything better. She waited.

Larry coughed and pounded his chest.

"You could at least tell me where you traveled to," she prodded, "What important government business kept you from seeing your son? Witness protection program? Was it to protect us? I've come up with some good stories myself over the years."

"Edna," he said, when he could breathe again, "Do you remember when I used to tell you I wanted to take you to the moon and the stars? The farthest reaches of the universe? Do you remember that I told you we would go to those places? That we were mated forever?"

"Yes," Enda said. The rasping bubbling sound in his voice was distracting and uncomfortable.

"I've been to some of those places," he answered. He coughed again for a few seconds. He had to take out his handkerchief and cover his mouth.

"Without me," Edna said flatly, "seems like you broke your promise."

"I've come back to take you now," Larry said, "To all those places.

"You and I must go to the stars Edna," he said, "We must visit the galaxies. It's only the next little bit that will be hard. But it will be hard." He wheezed and coughed the words out, detracting from any romantic feeling they might have evoked. He checked his watch, following the hands and muttering something to himself.

Enda closed her eyes for a moment. This was the end of her love story. Her lover had finally come back, and he was a lunatic. A dying lunatic. Her story was a tragedy. No. A dark comedy. She wasn't important enough to be tragic.

When she opened her eyes again, Larry was moving the hand of his watch, "Time to go," he said. He coughed and shivered, a slow shiver that shook him from his feet all the way up to his head. He dropped his hat and groaned. He clutched his side.

With alarm, Edna saw that twilight was falling in the wood. The sun slanted through the trees and fell directly along the leaf covered ground. The sky above was fading to purple. Was that the moon peering out from behind a cloud?

"Time to go where?" asked Edna, "How did it get so dark?"

Suddenly the sun disappeared, and a few tiny pinpricks of stars appeared at the very edges of the sky where moonlight faded.

Edna felt a chill creeping up her back.

"There is no time now," Larry said. He coughed and shivered, "It will happen quickly."

"What's going to happen quickly, Larry?" she asked. She pulled away, "What's going on? I just came up here to hear an explanation of why you left me and didn't come back. And if you can't give me that..."

The trees were receding into darkness. A cloud drifted across the moon. She wasn't sure she could find her way back down the hill without breaking an ankle.

Larry reached for her hand.

Edna stood up. She put her hands on her hips. It was time to put an end to this silliness. Larry was obviously insane. She couldn't believe Carl had just dropped him with her. When she found Carl...

She found that her legs were aching from sitting down so long. Standing up sent deep tracers of pain from her hip into her feet. The air was growing chill for summer. He could sit here on a log all night if he wanted to. Edna was going home.

A cloud slid from the face of the moon, suddenly illuminating the clearing.

"Now you listen to me Larry," she started. Then she noticed his ear.

"Larry, your ear," she said. "Oh my God! Your ear...It's slipped sideways."

Larry shook himself and put his hand to his ear and moved it around a bit, "Better?" he asked.

"No," Edna said gasping, "Worse."

He had pulled the ear down close to his chin.

Two things occurred to her at once, the first was that she should run. The second was that this must be a dream, because her feet did not want to move. They felt like lead. And they were so hot.

Larry stood up and stumbled toward her. She couldn't help staring at his ear...there was a line of crusted blood going all the way around it and a tear in the skin behind it. From the tear, something blue was oozing out. Edna gasped and stumbled backwards.

"Oh my God, Larry, what's happening?" she asked, "Tell me what's happening right now." She tried in vain to pick up her heavy feet, to get away.

He held out his hand, "Help me Edna. Don't leave me," he coughed again and this time a little blue liquid lingered on his lips. His nose began to bleed. There was blood dripping from it mixed with a shimmering blue fluid, like liquid light, "We have to go together. It's too late."

She tried to turn her now heavy upper body from Larry to the path behind them but found she couldn't move herself. He coughed again. Blue liquid spewed out. Smoke rose from the leaves where the droplets splashed.

"Larry! Tell me what's happening right now," she demanded. She put her hands in front of her to keep him away. She tried again to move her feet.

"We are mated Edna," he said, "We will become one. You and I will go on together now. I'm sorry. The choice is immovable on this timeline."

"Larry! What are you talking about?" Edna said, "I don't want to go with you!" Her mouth hurt. It felt heavy and stiff.

Larry fell forward and grabbed her skirt with his hand. He clutched it tightly in an attempt to either pull himself up or to keep her from leaving. Edna shrieked and grabbed his hand to remove it from her skirt.

She found herself holding the hand...and only the hand. It had come off Larry's arm. She stared at it.

"Don't leave me Edna," he said, "Sit with me. You can't go far from me. We are dissipating...together."

Edna threw the hand at him and screamed. Larry crawled toward it. With the hand he had left, he tried jamming the loose hand back on. Blood and blue liquid dripped from the end of his arm.

"Not much longer now Edna," he said. He was talking in a hoarse whisper.

Edna stood staring at the man in front of her. A fine line of blue liquid was beginning to drip from his eye.

"Come here to me. Please?" Larry said. He'd given up trying to reattach the hand and it lay on the log next to him, moving like a dying fish, throwing phosphorescent blue liquid like water.

Edna watched the blue ooze out of his wrist. Thin trickles of blue were coming from his eyes and ears and mouth. After a moment, the blue liquid ran down his chin and wherever it touched, left a crack in his skin. The blue light was leaking onto his clothes, burning though where it touched.

But the mouth still worked the cracking lips, "Come Edna," he whispered. "Come to me Edna. Sit with me."

Edna willed herself to move backwards. She must find her way down the hillside. Larry held out his one hand. It was cracking, emitting the blue ooze that was almost liquid light. The dead leaves on the ground glowed weirdly in the evanescence of the blue fluid.

She felt a burning pain in her foot. She looked down. Blue liquid was oozing around the top of her shoes.

"Am I dying?" Edna asked in a whisper. Her chest felt hot and tight. Her hands were sore. Her whole body was too small. The heat inside her was cracking her skin and bones.

Larry nodded, and his nose fell off, behind it was blue light. "Yes," he whispered, "And being born."

"Come with me, sit with me," he said, and his bottom lip fell off.

"Will it hurt?" Edna asked.

"Yes," whispered Larry and three of his teeth fell to the forest floor.

"Good," said Edna. She made up her mind. With a supreme effort, she crawled into his lap. Larry was right. It hurt. And Edna was glad.

The Sheriff's Tale

Hattie stood in the kitchen, the small of her back pressed into the corner of the countertops next to the refrigerator. She was holding an enormous black cat tightly against her chest. She had one arm under his tail, the other wrapped tightly around his heavy chest. Sheriff Martin Henry, her husband, stood at the far end of the table, the bulk of his body between herself and the kitchen door. He was in uniform and his coat made his shoulders appear wide and blocky. She thought briefly about how very square he was and realized that she'd always wished he were a few inches taller. She didn't think about that for long because his service revolver was pointed at her. That was the thing that mostly occupied her mind in the moment. But it was such an uncomfortable and unpleasant thing that her brain decided not to settle on it, instead flitting about trying to find other thoughts to land on. The gun was an object she'd seen a million times before – on the nightstand, in his holster, on the seat of his car. As she stared down its barrel, she thought that the reality of *gun* doesn't register until you look at the thing from the business end. This skimmed across her mind as a point of intellectual interest, another attempt to deflect the reality of the shiny implement of death at the other end of the kitchen. She wondered vaguely if the end of that revolver would be the last thing she would see. She tried not looking at it for a moment. The kitchen looked oddly normal except for Martin standing in it, pointing the gun at her. The clock ticked, trying to lighten the mood perhaps. The yellow rag rug by the kitchen sink looked absurdly cheerful. The jar of pink, round, tulips curved gracefully over the blue and white crock, maddeningly hopeful.

"Put the cat down, Hattie," Martin said. The ease of his voice, his deadly calm, as if he were addressing a suspect, rattled her. More than that, it made her angry.

"No, Martin," she said, "I will not let you shoot this cat. You're insane." Her voice was not calm. It trembled on the edge of tears. This further pissed her off. She did not want him to see how frightened she was.

"Put him down, Hattie," he said again, "You don't know what he is."

"Are you going to shoot me too, Martin?" she asked.

"You're going to put the cat down," he said, "Then I'm going to shoot the cat. That's the way it's going to be. Just set him down and move away."

Hattie heard a rushing in her ears. She couldn't afford to pass out right now. God only knew how that would end. Her hands shook, but still she clung to the animal in her arms. She was surprised that he hadn't panicked and run, but he rested against her chest purring, seemingly oblivious to the trouble they were in. He was a remarkable animal. He was also heavy, and her arms were starting to tremble from holding him.

"Richard will be here in a few minutes," she said, "I called him, Martin. He won't let you do this."

She could see Martin clench his jaw, "You shouldn't have done that, Hattie."

"He'll be here any minute," she said. She was more hopeful than certain.

"You'd better hope not," Martin said. He was starting to sweat now. Maybe he wasn't as calm as she thought, "I'm telling you Hattie that animal is from Hell. If you don't put him down, I can't guarantee what will happen."

Martin was getting blurry and for a moment she couldn't figure out why, then she realized she was crying.

"You don't understand, Martin," she said, "You don't understand."

She heard the sounds of tires in the driveway next to the house and then she saw Deputy Richard Smith at the kitchen door. She slid with the cat onto the floor, in the corner between the sink and the refrigerator and then cat, kitchen and everything, twisted into a long dark tunnel.

Hattie met the cat in question on a Tuesday – one week after Father Dingle, the priest at St. Bartholomew's, insisted that Hell had broken out of the supply closet in the choir room of the historic stone church. Margie, the church secretary, backed up this claim. They said demons had flown up through a crack in the floor of the supply closet, burning and trashing the choir room, then burst through the basement windows into the church cemetery. According to Maggie and Father Dingle, the demons had attacked Alan Cunningham, the choir director, who had been knocked unconscious during the incident.

According to Hattie's husband, Sheriff Henry, Deputy Smith and Fire Chief Marsh, the damage to the choir room, the busted practice piano, the shredded confetti of the Easter music, the odd smell of burnt match ends, the remains of greenish smoke and mud could all be attributed to a pipe bomb or bombs thrown through the basement window. They did not discuss any evidence for or against this hypothesis with the townspeople. Whether they had evidence or whether they were simply trying to keep everyone calm was up for debate. Even Hattie wasn't certain what Martin really thought.

It certainly was a puzzler. While there was considerable damage to the church basement, upon inspection, there was no visible hole or crack in the floor of the supply closet. When Alan Cunningham returned from the hospital, he couldn't corroborate the priest's story. He had to admit that he couldn't clearly remember what happened. The only lasting damage Alan had was a circular wound on his neck that was already beginning to heal. Almost miraculous, said Dr. Ford, who attributed the injury to shrapnel. Margie and Father Dingle both insisted that they had seen one of the creatures from the portal in the choir room bite Alan's neck in that very spot. After patching up Alan's neck, Dr. Ford had prescribed both Father Dingle and Margie some pills.

Almost every citizen in Whistlestop was ruminating on this story. Most of them were leaning towards the official version because it was awfully uncomfortable to believe that the church was sitting on a portal to Hell. Of course, there were a number of people in town who thoroughly enjoyed believing in Hell, no doubt about that. Father Dingle's story was very attractive on some level. But most people liked to think that Hell was largely a problem for other people in other towns, or at least the kind of people who went to the Pop-A-Top bar down on the edge of town on a Sunday instead of church. They were willing to believe that some demon possessed person, perhaps an atheist or a Satanist had caused the damage. They were not quite prepared to believe Hell had been allowed to tunnel up and into their historically significant church building. And yet...there was the damage. The Easter music was done for. The choir room looked like a war zone. Plastic covered the basement windows. Yellow police tape flared across the building like a flamboyant spider web.

Theories were batted around the barber shop and discussed everywhere from Joe's Diner on the Square, to the Pop-A-Top on the far end of town. William Robert Jackson, known to his friends as Billy Bob, a high school dropout and Pop-A-Top bar-tender who spent his spare time reading the old paperback science fiction collection his father had left him and watching re-runs of every iteration of Star Trek, theorized that Hell or at least any portal to Hell might not exist at a stable point on the space time continuum as we know it and therefore might appear and disappear seemingly at random. This theory was too complex and didn't really fit the theological world-view of Whistlestop. It didn't catch on. There were other theories, less scientific.

Someone at Joe's Diner theorized that Margie and Father Dingle had simply seen a vision of Hell, like the guy who wrote the book of Revelations. Mary Jo Baker pointed out that this did not explain the state of the practice piano. Ginger Price, her day waitress, suggested that maybe the vision had been triggered by the pipe bomb which might have been set off by a Satanist. At any rate, the story of the demons hung in the air, the decision to believe Father Dingle caught in the balance between excitement and discomfort.

It was in this atmosphere of suspicious exhilaration that Hattie met the cat. She was walking home from the grocery store. Hattie walked to Barton and Smith's Grocery on Tuesdays. It was only about six blocks from her house. Hattie was a tall woman with short hair, a little gray if you looked hard, otherwise what her mother had always called dishwater blonde. She would turn forty-eight in May. She was pleasant to look at and almost pretty when she smiled. She had a reputation as being friendly enough, but not too friendly. The kind of woman who would show up at your Uncle Joe's funeral visitation with a casserole, but not press you for details as to how much Jack Daniels he'd consumed before they found him under the riding lawn mower.

Hattie liked to walk to the grocery store. She liked to see what was blooming; she liked the exercise; and she liked fresh ingredients for dinner, besides with both kids away at college, she didn't need to keep as much food around the house. Martin, her husband, told her walking was a waste of time. Martin didn't like to waste time. He bought her a chest freezer and put it in the garage, so she could buy in bulk when she went to Costco in Midtown. She had to admit that many times she been grateful that Martin was more practical than she was. He was always thinking about how to make things easier for her and the kids. She was a bit of a dreamer. She thought their personalities complemented one another perfectly. They often joked that each one of them had half the brain and together they were a whole person.

Spring had come to Whistlestop the Tuesday she met the cat but seemed equivocal about remaining. The warm sun invited Hattie to take off her windbreaker and red wool scarf, but a brittle breeze begged to differ. For once, she almost agreed with her husband that it would have been better to drive to the store after she'd zipped and unzipped her jacket and wound and unwound her scarf at least six times before she reached the square.

On that Tuesday, there was another reason Hattie was almost sorry she'd walked into town. Everyone wanted to know if Hattie knew anything about the case at St. Bartholomew. Had Sheriff Henry arrested anyone? Did he have suspects? Was Alan Cunningham, the choir director, going to be all right? Did the Sheriff think there was anything to Father Dingle's story about demons? Hattie repeatedly told everyone that Alan had been released, no she didn't know anything, if she did she wouldn't be able to say, and no...she was pretty sure that none of his suspects were supernatural.

Other than the questions of her fellow citizens, things seemed fairly normal. Even the church looked more pitiable than frightening in the bright spring sunlight, covered in bright yellow police tape, with thick cloudy plastic on the basement windows. She stopped to admire Isabelle's white Thalia narcissus. The sun teased out their sweet, earthy fragrance. She stopped briefly to admire the butter yellow daffodils and bright pink early tulips on the lawn in the middle of the square. As she always did on Tuesday, she went to Joe's Diner on the Square. She slid across the worn red vinyl into the corner booth up front, where the sun spilled from both sides onto the gray Formica tabletop. Mary Jo Baker brought out a slawburger all-the-way and a diet cherry coke without even asking. Hattie pulled out her book, a mystery set in India, a comfortable distance from Whistlestop and Knobb Mountain. It was nice to escape sometimes. She hunched over it to send the signal that she was too focused on the book to answer questions about St. Bartholomew's.

She bought more than she expected at Barton's, including a six-pound chicken that was on sale, and a half-gallon of milk. She planned to roast the chicken and have enough left for chicken salad and a chicken pot pie. Maybe one of the kids would be in from school that weekend. The weight of the canvas bag on her shoulder made her wardrobe adjustments elaborate and time consuming. She had to stop and set her purse and groceries on a park bench while she unzipped her coat, and once more on the winter scraps table in front of Cotton's Notions and Fabrics to zip it back up. Only a few blocks from home, Hattie found herself sweating again, a combination of exertion and the sun's sudden decision to get the upper hand of the weather. She set her bag down on the stone retaining wall in front of Irma Watson's gray stone Georgian, behind the substantial wall of hollies by the iron gate. She didn't want to answer any of Irma's questions. It had only been a week since the incident at the church and Irma, head of the Altar Guild at St. Bartholomew's, had already expressed her disdain for the pace of the investigation in a letter to the editor.

While she was unzipping her jacket, she heard a slight rustling in the holly bush. Fearing that Irma was out walking her dreadful Jack Russells, Hattie stood still, hoping Irma wouldn't see her. As she stood, nearly holding her breath, waiting for the shrill sound of barking on the other side, she saw a pair of lemon-yellow eyes staring out from a dark hollow in the center of the thick, twisted holly branches. Initially, they appeared to be attached to nothing, floating in the inky shadows. Then the darkness surrounding the eyes pushed forward, oozing into the sunlight and taking the form of a cat, a massive animal, with a wide head, and thick ruff falling away from his chin. His coat was long, thick, and shaggy, a vague matte black, that faded into shadow on the ends. He was very difficult to see even in the bright spring light. Tufts of hair stood out of his ears. The left ear was ragged with battle scars.

The animal moved toward Hattie slowly, sinuously, curving himself through the wrought iron fence. When he had fully conjured himself out of the shrubs, he stopped. He walked to the grocery bag and patted it with his paw. When she didn't move, he patted it again. He made a small mewing sound. He put his head into the bag and grabbed a package of ham with his teeth and then released it again and looked at her.

She reached into the bag slowly and carefully to keep from startling him into biting her or running away. He did neither. He waited patiently for her to open the ham and give him a piece. He ate it neatly and quickly and patted her hand for another. Afterwards, he walked up to her and rubbed his massive head on her hand, purring so violently that he vibrated.

"Where on earth did you come from?" she asked him, rubbing his torn left ear. His only answer was his deep rumbling purr.

"I had a cat that looked a lot like you when I was young" she told him as she hoisted the grocery bag from the stone wall.

The cat stood gazing at her calmly.

"I would invite you home with me, but Martin does not care for cats," she said. The cat didn't answer. He turned to groom his long, curving tail, as if to let her know that she was free to leave, he had other things on his schedule.

"Watch out for Irma and her nasty little dogs," Hattie warned him, but he seemed unconcerned and continued cleaning himself.

As an afterthought, she said, "I really, really wish I could just sit around and pet you all afternoon." He looked up from cleaning his tail abruptly, stared at her and then blinked as if acknowledging her statement.

"Maybe I'll see you around," she said.

She didn't have long to wait. She set the bag of groceries on the back stoop and while she was fishing for her keys, she felt something pushing against her leg. She looked down and there was the cat.

"What on earth are you doing here?" she asked. He didn't answer. She bent down to pet him, and he put his paws up and crawled around her shoulder. He curved around her neck, perfectly balanced, as if they'd practiced the routine.

"My cat used to do that," she said, "He used to do just that very thing." She couldn't dislodge him from her neck, so she opened the door and walked inside the kitchen. He jumped onto the floral tablecloth her mother-in-law had given her. The elder Mrs. Henry felt it was "country" to have a bare table and she'd made a habit of gifting Hattie table cloths and table runners, usually in colors that exactly didn't match Hattie's kitchen.

She let him sit there. She and Martin had always agreed that there would be no pets. But she certainly wasn't trying to make this cat a pet. He was a guest. He held one leg up like a ballet dancer, grooming himself. He was comfortable with her hospitality, amusing himself as she put up the groceries.

When she was done, they stood gazing at each other for a moment.

"You really shouldn't be in here," she said, "Martin would flip out."

He stared back at her calmly, blinking his lemon-yellow eyes.

She looked at the clock. Only two thirty and Martin surely wouldn't be home until six thirty or so. He'd been late almost every night for the last week or so with all that mess at St. Bartholomew's.

"Oh, all right," she said, "Just for a few minutes."

She picked up the enormous cat and walked with him to the overstuffed chair in the living room.

"Heaven's sakes, you must weigh twenty pounds," she said.

She rubbed his head and fondled his torn ear.

"You're remarkably friendly," she said, "I wonder why I've never seen you around."

The cat licked the skin between her thumb and forefinger with his sandpaper tongue.

"I found my cat, the one you remind me of, by the mailbox when I got off the bus. I think I was in sixth grade," she told the cat, "My father made me name him Temporary because he said I had to find him a new home. The joke was on Daddy. I had that cat from the time he was a shrieking little ball of fur, until I went away to college," she told the cat in her lap. He had her hand between his paws now, still licking away with his raspy pink tongue.

"Of course, I didn't know Martin didn't like cats while we were dating," she sighed, "It never came up. We were in college." This felt like an apology, whether to Temporary, the cat in her lap, or cats in general she did not know.

The sun poured in the tall living room window and a syrupy warmth filled the air in spite of the chilly breeze rattling the windows now and then. Hattie felt her eyes growing heavy.

"He was probably happier on the farm, don't you think? The cat, I mean," she asked the cat in her lap, "He was a big guy like you. Our first apartment would have been too small for him and Lord only knows how he would have felt about a crying baby. I suppose it was for the best."

The cat stretched out and needled her sweater with his claw for a second and then curled back into a ball, "My father was actually kind of fond of him by then. Said he didn't mind him staying. Said he kept the rabbits out of the pole beans."

The cat was beginning to snore a little and Hattie put her head back and thought about the laundry she should be doing. The kitchen floor needed mopping. She'd promised herself she would pack up that junk in the garage for Goodwill. The chicken needed to be in the oven no later than three thirty as big as it was. Her eyes were heavy though. She supposed she could close them for just a second.

When Hattie woke up it was twenty after four. The cat was still curled on her lap, snoring a whiffling, contented snore. She jumped up from the chair, spilling him to the floor. He didn't seem terribly startled. He stretched his front feet in front of him and yawned.

"I'm sorry," she said, "You have to go out."

He didn't protest when she set him out on the stoop. He stretched again and then slowly ambled towards the back hedge.

She hadn't started dinner. She hadn't washed any socks or underwear for Martin and the tablecloth was covered with fur. She sighed, balled up the tablecloth and rummaged through the refrigerator to see what she could make for dinner.

"What's with the grilled ham and cheese and tomato soup?" Martin asked when they sat down at the table, "I thought you were walking to Barton's today?"

"I forgot to put the chicken in," she said, "We can always have it tomorrow, then I'll make pot pie."

"I suppose so. It's been a helluva day is all." He sighed and picked up his sandwich. He dipped the corner of it in his soup. It dripped red sauce onto the table.

"What happened to the table cloth?" he asked.

"It's in the laundry," she said, "I didn't put another one on because I kind of liked the way the maple looked just plain. It's just the color of the wildflower honey in the window of Barton's." She ran her finger over the wormy grain, admiring it.

"Won't look good for long if it gets scratched up," Martin said "Hey, can you get me some more tea?"

"How was your day?" she asked, as she poured more sweet tea into his glass.

"How do you think it was?" Martin said, "Richard and I have questioned nearly everyone in town and we're no closer to an answer than we were the day we started. Not only that, I've had at least three old ladies stop by the station to pray over me to protect me from demons."

"Watch out for Harriet Davis," Hattie said as she sat back down, "She goes to that nondenominational Bible Church over in Putnam. She prayed over Harold when he had that bad leg last year, poured oil on his head. He said he had to crutch around all day with a greasy head. Angel nearly slipped in some oil near the cash register." Harold and Angel were the proprietors of The Laughing Pink Elephant, a local antique store.

"If I see Harriet, I'm locking the station door. Lord, I wish some of these people would get some practical religion in 'em," said Martin, "A little less drinking and coveting of other people's wives. A little more minding their own business. Then the old ladies could quit pestering God on my behalf."

"You'd be out of a job," Hattie replied, smiling.

"That sounds pretty good to me today," Martin shook his head.

"Is Alan okay?" Hattie asked, "I heard that he was released from the hospital a few days ago."

"He's fine, I guess," Martin replied, "That cut on his neck is getting better but he's having some dizzy spells. Dr. Ford couldn't really find anything wrong with him. Just the after effects of being knocked unconscious I guess. His sister came to get him. She lives over on the other side of Midtown. She's going to let him stay with her for a few weeks. Won't be any choir practice until they get the new windows in anyway."

"I hope he doesn't have any lasting damage," Hattie said.

"I talked to him before he left. He seems fine to me," he answered, "A little addled but then I sometimes think that's normal for Alan. How was your day? Other than forgetting to put the chicken in the oven."

"I saw a big black cat out by Irma Johnson's house," Hattie said, almost biting her tongue as soon as she said it. It didn't seem like a topic that would soothe Martin.

"Huge black cat? Kinda scruffy looking?" asked Martin, surprising her.

"Yes," said Hattie, "Why?"

"I had a run-in with a big old black cat just this morning. Must have been the same cat. I've never seen a cat that size. A few of the braver ladies from the altar guild went over to the choir room see if anything could be salvaged. Irma heard something rustling around in the basement and thought the vandals might be back."

"If anyone would fight a pack of demons over a choir robe, it would be Irma," Hattie said, "Did Father Dingle show up?".

"He's made himself a nervous wreck. Still talking about demons. At the very least, I wish he'd shut up about it. He's got the whole town on edge and I can't see that it's doing anyone a lick of good," Martin answered.

"Oh dear, poor man," said Hattie.

"Dr. Ford gave him some pills. Maybe they'll settle him down," said Martin.

"So, what about the cat?" Hattie asked.

"Well, after Irma says she hears something in the basement rustling around behind the choir room door, we hear something fall down. I go in with my gun drawn. And there's that old cat, on its hind feet trying to get in the door of the store room closet, scratching at the doorknob. Looked for all the world like he was trying to turn it."

"I wonder what he was up to?" Hattie said.

"I'll be damned if I know," said Martin, "Anyway, he saw us and took off like a streak up and out through the plastic on the windows. Guess that's how he got in, in the first place. He's lucky I didn't shoot him. That would have solved the problem."

"Oh, for goodness sakes, Martin!" Hattie said. She thumped her spoon into her bowl and splashed the remains of her tomato soup onto the table.

"What?" he asked, "He scared the crap out of us. Wish they'd get those windows in. By the way, if you see him again, let me know."

"The cat?" she asked

"No, Hattie. I'm going to have Animal Control pick up Father Dingle," he shook his head, "Yes. The cat."

"Why would you have animal control pick him up? Seems to me that once they get the windows in, the problem will be solved. He probably just chased a rat down there."

"In the meantime, he doesn't need to get in and scratch the pews and spray everything. You know how tomcats are," Martin said.

Hattie got up and put her dishes in the sink with perhaps too much emphasis. The spoon slid out of the bowl and clattered on the porcelain.

"Oh, c'mon Hattie!" Martin said, with a sigh, "Why are you always making me feel like the bad guy? It's a cat. I've never understood why you're so foolish about cats."

Hattie stood rinsing the dishes and the soup pan, her back to Martin, "For goodness sakes, Martin! It's not foolish to care about the welfare of animals."

"Maybe you should consider my welfare occasionally. Isn't this the second time we've had soup and sandwiches this week? And it's what, Tuesday?" he asked, "I had to go on an expedition to the basement in my pajamas this morning looking for a pair of underwear."

Hattie wiped down the sink and said nothing.

"Good God," Martin said, "I'm just telling you about my day, and you can't spare me as much sympathy as you can a stray animal."

"Strangely, the cat did not complain to me about its laundry," Hattie said, "Maybe that's why I felt such a sudden fondness for it."

"All I can say is do not bring that cat home," Martin said.

Her back stiffened and she turned to face him. She put both hands on the sink behind her, "Martin, why on earth would I think that you would allow me to have a cat after twenty-five years."

"For god's sake woman," he pushed his chair back from the table, "Don't say allow, like anybody could tell you what to do. I told you I didn't like cats before we were married."

"You told me you didn't like cats three days before the wedding, Martin," she said, "I had to call my mother and beg her to keep my cat."

"They liked that cat fine," he replied, "It wasn't a big deal."

Hattie stared at him. She could feel her face flushing, "It was a big deal Martin. It was a very big deal to me."

"Good God, Hattie," he said, "Where did this come from? It's been twenty-five goddamn years. You know what? I really don't need this right now. I think I'm going out to the garage to stain those shelves."

He scraped the chair back, banged it back under the table and stomped off.

"Fine" said Hattie, "Sounds like an excellent idea."

Instead of wiping down the table, she stood staring out the window for a moment, wondering what had just happened.

It took two days, gravy and biscuits for breakfast one day, pancakes the next, a roast chicken and a pot pie to return them to speaking terms. Hattie noted with resignation that the effort seemed to be mostly on her part. Then again, she had to keep telling himself, Martin's job had never been so stressful. She couldn't quite forgive herself for deciding to argue with him in the middle of this mess.

It was Thursday night when Martin finally rolled over and put his arms around her, his hand inside her pajama shirt. Hattie had just relaxed into sleep when the phone on the nightstand rang. Martin groaned.

"Jesus," he muttered, "I knew this would happen. I wish that old man would shut up about his demons."

The phone call was from Isabelle Graham, possessor of Hattie's favorite white Thalia daffodils. She was a sixty-five-year old woman of boundless, sleepless energy who lived alone across from the church. She had looked up the Sheriff's home phone number from the church directory, since she wasn't certain that she had an emergency on her hands. She was certain that she'd seen someone wandering around in the graveyard at St. Bartholomew's. If the Sheriff didn't want to come over or send someone, maybe he would like her to take her flashlight and check it out herself?

He assured her that he would not like that at all.

"I'm worried Martin," Hattie said as he pulled on his uniform pants, "I hate for you to go out there on your own. Want me to ride with you?"

"Whoever is there will probably be gone by the time I get there," he answered, "I'll probably just do a drive-by, just to keep Isabelle in her house. If it looks dangerous or if someone is there, I'll call Richard or one of the other guys. I promise."

"Be careful."

"It's my job, Hattie. Fussing over me doesn't make it any easier," he said, frowning.

"I worry Martin," she said, "Because I love you."

He leaned over and kissed her forehead, "I will do my level best not to be killed."

There was no way Hattie could sleep after Martin left. She got up, wrapped herself in her white house coat and put the kettle on. The moon fell through the window, puddling on the maple table top, moonlight and wormholes forming ghosts in the woodgrain. She looked out the window and saw a stiff wind shaking blossoms off her weeping cherry, flinging them towards the window.

Just as she poured the hot water over the teabag, she heard something thud against the door. Her heart nearly skipped a beat. She poured boiling water onto the counter top. Thud, thud, thud. She stood perfectly still, barely breathing. Then she heard a soft meow.

She walked to the door and opened it. There was her friend. He put out a paw and touched the edge of her robe. She sat on the stoop and let him leap into her lap. The wind was strong, but it was warmer than it had been for the past few days. Probably a spring storm moving in.

"Good Lord, you almost scared me to death," she said, "Glad I'm not superstitious. A big black cat showing up on a night like this. You'd better not come in. Martin and I have already had a big fight about you. Did you know that?"

She picked him up and held him against her for a moment. She felt him purring.

"Do you know what I wish?" she asked the cat. He didn't respond. She went on, "I wish that Martin would find someone to put in jail for this stupid thing at the church. Maybe then everyone would settle down." The cat looked up at her and blinked.

She was still sitting on the stoop with the cat in her lap when she heard the phone ring.

The Sheriff pulled up to the graveyard and parked the car by the iron gate. He looked across the street and saw the light in Isabelle's front window. She was pressed against the glass. She waved. He sighed and turned off the car. He would have to go in and look around. He turned on the flashlight, even though the moon was so bright he almost didn't need it. He walked into the little cemetery and shone the light to his left, against the basement windows. The light seeped into the thick, opaque plastic. Nothing. He shone the light straight ahead. It glanced across the rows of old tombstones by the moss covered gray wall at the back by the shrubbery. It picked out the eerie death's head on old Maggie Allan's tombstone, which bore an uncanny resemblance to Maggie as she appeared in life.

He took a few more steps into the graveyard, under the ancient spreading maple, shining the light to his right, over the tops of the new gravestones. He'd just satisfied himself that there was nothing amiss when he heard a sudden rustling in the tree above him. A shower of leaves fell on his head. Startled, he flipped the flashlight upward. For a split second, the flashlight caught the outline of a dark shape, then flicked against a set of glowing yellow-green eyes. Before he could properly assess the creature, there was a loud crack. Next thing he could remember, he was on the ground, blinking, rubbing his head. He felt a trickle of blood over his right eyebrow and a sharp pain on the side of his neck.

Hattie picked up her phone.

"Hattie," she heard Isabelle's voice, "Stay calm."

That, Hattie thought, was the worst phrase in the world to use if you actually wanted someone to stay calm.

"Is he alive?" Hattie asked. Her stomach tightened.

"He's alive. A branch fell on his head over at the cemetery. The wind probably knocked it down. Damned fool refuses to go to the emergency room. I reckon I'll bring him home. It's not that far to walk back over for the car when he feels better."

Hattie got up early and took him breakfast in bed.

"Waffles and bacon!" she said cheerfully, "Don't get syrup on the comforter."

"I'm not an invalid," he said, frowning.

"So, what happened?" she asked, after he was done eating. She attempted to inspect the cut over his eye. He had an egg sized knot above the cut and a bandage on his neck. He pulled back from her, covering his neck with his hand.

"Ow," he said, "It's no big deal, but I'm still sore."

"Sorry," she said, and moved away.

"Somebody should trim up that old maple," he said, "A dead branch like that could kill someone whose head wasn't hard as mine."

"There was a strong wind last night," Hattie said, "Quite a storm too after you got home. It took me awhile to get to sleep."

Martin swung his legs to the floor. Hattie had never known him to take a sick day. No matter what. She sighed. He was going into the station. She picked up his plate from the nightstand and turned to walk out.

"Hattie," he said as she reached the door. She turned.

"I saw something in that tree," he said.

"What are you talking about, Martin?" she asked.

"I saw a pair of eyes in that tree," he said, "Yellow eyes."

"What do you think it was?" Hattie asked, "An owl maybe, or a buzzard?"

"It wasn't a bird," he answered, "I only saw it for a second before the branch fell. But it wasn't a bird."

Hattie didn't respond.

"It looked like a big cat, to be honest. Maybe like that cat I saw in the church basement. Too dark to tell for sure. Whatever it was, when the limb fell, it fell on me too. Scratched my neck and ran off."

"I'm sure it wasn't the cat. For goodness sakes," Hattie said. She was really was quite sure it wasn't the cat – unless he could be in two places at once – but she really didn't want to explain it to Martin. All she said was the same thing she'd told the cat the night before, "I wish you'd figure out who was responsible for that mess at the church. Maybe people would settle down and quit calling you out at night."

The same storm that brought the maple branch down on the tough, square head of Sheriff Henry, left behind a fresh washed sun and shell-colored clouds, as pretty as an Easter post card. The apricot buds of the peach trees were opening against a clear blue dome of sky. The azaleas unfurled themselves, the irises started to bloom. Even the fairy roses by the walk seemed to have made handfuls of tight pink buds overnight.

Hattie went out into the garden early to weed her flower beds after the rain. As Martin walked out the front, the cat appeared from beneath the white rhododendron in the back garden. He spent the morning next to Hattie as she weeded her flower beds. Around eleven, Hattie put on her sneakers and headed down to the square. She was out of milk and she'd seen a length of blue cloth at Cotton's she thought would make a nice skirt. The cat followed along behind. He popped into shrubs and occasionally dashed off between buildings after birds or lizards. When she went into Joe's he walked into the dark alley between the buildings and began washing his paws.

She was sitting in her booth at Joe's Diner on the Square, reading her book, when she looked out the window in time to see an ambulance zip past the police station and take a right onto Washington, a quiet tree-lined street, of older, stately houses. She waited for them to wail right out of town, but instead they stopped, obviously very close. She sat up in the booth and tried in vain to fathom what was happening. In a few minutes, the phone at the diner rang and Mary Jo grabbed her to-go pad, pulled a pencil out from behind her ear, and picked up the receiver.

Hattie heard Mary Jo saying, "It's what now? At the Elephant? Do they know who it is?"

Mary Jo's face was pale. She dropped her pencil. She turned away from the cash register and retreated as far as the phone cord would allow toward the kitchen. Unfortunately, Hattie could still hear every word. She wished she couldn't because obviously something terrible was happening.

Mary Jo was listening carefully now, then she said, "Sarah Lawson? Are you sure? Oh Lord Almighty. I always knew she should've left that man."

The voice on the other line responded and then Mary Jo said, "I know they don't know who did it, but I bet you money it was Rodney. She's called the law on him before."

Mary Jo listened for another minute and then snorted, "Demons? You mean those evil spirits he's been drinking down at the Pop-A-Top? This time, it may be meth. His cousin Jimmy's a dealer. It's just too bad. That's all I have to say."

Mary Jo hung up the phone with a bang. She looked at Hattie, "Get ready to join the stampede over to the Elephant." That's what a lot of the townspeople called The Laughing Pink Elephant. "They've found a body."

"What?" Hattie asked, mid bite. She squeezed her patty melt a little too hard and meat and grilled onion shot out the back in a big gloopy mess.

Mary Jo said, "They've found little Sarah Lawson stabbed and stuffed into a closet over at the Elephant. After what happened over at the church, Lord only knows what you will find in a closet in this town anymore. I'm afraid to get my coat out of mine." She shook her head and looked past Hattie out the window.

"Sarah Lawson?" asked Hattie. She was trying to place her.

"Waitress over at the Pop-A-Top," Mary Jo said, "It was the husband. Mark my words. That kid never was a lick of good. Wouldn't be the first time he's hurt her. Plus, he used to do janitor work over at the Elephant. Had a key." She pursed her lips then smacked the rag down hard. The frown faded, and she pulled a Kleenex out of her apron. She dabbed at her eyes.

"I went to school with her mama," she said, "Lord almighty, she is going to break her heart over this." She turned abruptly and walked back into the kitchen.

Sheriff Henry stood in the store room of the Laughing Pink Elephant, his handkerchief over his mouth. Deputy Smith was out front trying to keep the curious throng at a distance. Joe Benson, the only officer who knew how to use the camera, was taking pictures of the body. Sarah lay on the floor, pale and dead. Dead as dead could be. The Sheriff looked across the body to the torn screen on the window. It was probable that whoever stuffed Sarah into the closet had brought her through the door. The tear in the screen was only big enough to let in a few flies. Sheriff Henry looked through the window at the old apple tree behind the Laughing Pink Elephant. He frowned and squinted. There was a shadow in the middle of the tree, a compact darkness, right where the trunk split into gnarled green and pink branches. He squinted again. Was it the cat? It didn't quite look like a cat, but whatever it was, it was big and black.

He stepped forward and one of his officers put out an arm.

"Whoa," said Officer Taylor "You alright Sheriff? You're about to step right on the body."

The Sheriff shook his head and backed up blinking. The dark shape leapt from the tree to the ground and he couldn't see it from the window any more. He pushed past Deputy Smith and the crowd out front and hurried to the back of the building. There was nothing but sunlight on the wide green lawn. The apple tree was empty. It had to be the cat, he thought, What else could it be? Damn cat.

Deputy Smith came and stood next to him, "See anything?" he asked, "Footprints or anything?"

"No," he said, "Nothing back here."

He was still looking around vaguely. His hand went to his neck. It was hurting like crazy all the sudden.

"Maybe you oughta get Dr. Ford to look at that," Deputy Smith said.

"Who are you? My wife?" the Sheriff responded.

The deputy chuckled. "Angel and Harold say the husband had a key," he said, "Used to do janitor work here. Think we should go see him now? I've got the guys taking information from the tourist that found her."

"Yeah," the Sheriff said, shaking himself back to reality, "Angel says she overheard them fighting not too long ago. Says Rodney was threatening her. Let's go talk."

Sure enough, they found Rodney Lawson on his couch, head in his hands, crying, shirt covered in blood. There was a scratch under his eye, and several on his cheek. There was a wound on his neck, though the Sheriff thought to himself it looked older than the scratches, it had scabbed over good. His hand went to the bandage on his neck and he briefly thought about the night in the cemetery, but some darkness in his brain swallowed the memory. He shook his head to clear it.

Deputy Smith shook his head, "She fought back," he was saying, "Poor Sarah."

Rodney said he'd been so drunk the night before that he couldn't remember anything. They told him that Sarah was dead, that she'd been stabbed. He threw up.

There was one other thing that Deputy Smith and Sheriff Taylor found. The materials to make a pipe bomb. Rodney said that he and his cousin Jimmy had been picked up by the game warden the year before. Fishing with pipe bombs. Jimmy had cut out for Georgia in January because the DEA was after him. Rodney couldn't say for sure where he'd been on the day of the church bombing, or the night before either. It didn't look good for Rodney, and it sure looked like the Sheriff was going to solve two of the worst crimes in Whistlestop history with one arrest.

Hattie's sense of relief was not long-lived. That night Martin came into the table, freshly scrubbed and wearing jeans and a plaid shirt. Hattie hoped it was the cut above his eye and the bruise on his head that made him look so angry. He'd put a fresh bandage on his neck.

"Do you need some aspirin? You look like you might have a headache," she said.

Martin simply grunted in response.

As Hattie set the pot pie on the table, he said, "I know you can't tell the temperature anymore due to your hormones but maybe you should close that window. It'll kick the heat on in a minute."

Hattie bit her tongue and closed the window against the spring air. The curtains, which had been puffing cheerfully, fell dead against the glass panes.

"Guess you heard about Sarah Lawson," he said.

"Yes," she replied, "I was there when Angel called Mary Jo."

Martin dug into his pot pie and took a huge bite. "Damn," he said, "I burned my mouth. Shit."

"It just came out of the oven," Hattie said. Martin didn't respond. She finally tried, "I'm so sorry about Sarah. I hope arresting Rodney will put all this nonsense to rest."

"A woman is dead, Hattie," Martin said, "Solving the case won't do shit for her."

Hattie wasn't sure exactly how to respond to that, so she ate in silence.

Finally, Martin said, "Alan's sister called today. She had to take him back to the doctor. He won't sleep. He wants to play piano all day she says. When she asked him to stop he threw his music stand across the room. His doctor in Midtown thinks it's due to the concussion. Says sometimes patients get personality changes and anger issues. It's rare but it happens."

"That's too bad," Hattie answered, "Is there anything they can do about it?"

"Damned if I know," Martin said, "They're taking him for an MRI. I don't know what they'll do if they find out he's cracked. I don't even know why she called me." He rubbed his temples.

Hattie scooted peas and bits of chicken around on her plate.

"Oh," he said, looking up casually, "I also wanted to tell you something that I saw today. Something of interest to you, maybe. It was in that old apple tree out behind The Laughing Pink Elephant."

"What?" Hattie finally asked. He was apparently going to wait until she asked him.

"That black cat," he said, "Probably the same one I saw over at the church, hunched up in the tree like a shadow. He has a strange habit of showing up where something bad is happening."

Hattie didn't know how to respond.

"I would think you'd be too far away to tell," she said, "I mean that it was exactly that cat."

"What else would it be?" Martin responded, "He's the only cat that size I've seen around. He's enormous. Probably isn't one cat out of a thousand that size. We don't have monkeys around here. Dogs don't climb trees."

"Are you sure it wasn't a buzzard?" she asked, "You know I've seen a lot of them lately. They're big and dark."

"I think even from a distance, I can tell the difference between a large bird and a cat, Hattie," he said, "I'm not that far gone yet."

"Maybe it was one of Father Dingle's demons," she said, trying to keep her voice light.

"That's really funny, Hattie. Do you know what else I saw? Tonight, when I pulled into the drive?" he asked.

"No," Hattie said, but she was afraid she did, "What did you see?"

"I saw that same black cat sitting out in the back by our rhododendron," he said, "I ran it off."

"Maybe one of the neighbors is feeding it," Hattie said. She looked him square in the eye.

"I really don't care for cats, Hattie," he said, "You know that."

Hattie looked out the window for a moment, into the gathering dusk. She knew she should just let it go, but she said, "What can it hurt if he's outside?"

"I don't want him around," he said. He reached across the table and thumped another chunk of pot pie onto his plate, "I don't like him. I don't like cats."

"I just don't see how it can affect you," she said.

His jaw tightened. He dropped his fork in his plate. He pushed back his chair and held up his hands.

"You know what? I'm going over to the Pop-A-Top. There's a few more people over there I need to talk to. See if Rodney was over there at all around the time of the church bombing. Don't wait up." The door thudded shut behind him.

Hattie was still sitting at the table, when she heard something banging at the door and then a low meow.

She opened the door and the cat rubbed her legs, then stretched up putting his paws on her knees. She carried him to the mosaic tile table under the pergola. She rubbed her finger along the grout lines with one hand and held the cat in the other. Martin had made the table for her from some of her broken blue and white china. She watched the last bit of sunlight fade from the garden until only the ghost-white flowers of her rhododendron were visible.

She was wearing a pale blue tunic with a long tie at the neck and the cat slapped lazily at it. She shivered a little in the breeze and bent over him for warmth.

"Maybe it's me," she said, "I just don't feel like myself anymore now that the kids are gone. Maybe I'm the reason we don't get along. He just seems so pissed off all the time now."

The cat lifted both paws, chewing and tugging on the string to her shirt.

"I suppose I should send you away," she told him, "But why should I? You're not bothering anyone. You stay outside. You're not even here every day."

The garden was turning violet and a chill was settling. She pulled the cat closer. He captured the string on her shirt and began chewing on it.

"I just don't know what to do with him anymore," she pulled the string from his paws and tickled his nose with it, "I guess he's stressed. He didn't get like this when Wiley Rantham killed his brother over three dollars and a bottle of moonshine. And that was a whole lot bloodier. Wiley killed Abram with a pitchfork."

She sat still for a few minutes, comparing the Martin of ten years ago with the Martin of tonight. Maybe it was her. She had to admit she'd been a good bit less pliable since perimenopause had set in. But Martin hadn't exactly been a prize either.

"Men are so much trouble," she sighed as she nuzzled the cat, "Sometimes I wish I wasn't married at all. That it was just me." She stopped to tickle his nose, "And a cat, of course. Just sometimes. Like tonight."

The cat gazed at her serenely and blinked.

They sat there together until the moon had risen over them. Hattie was wondering if she should get a sweater or maybe just go inside when she heard the car pulling back up into the driveway. The cat was gone in a flash.

She didn't move. She saw Martin walk in the house. She'd left the kitchen lights on. She watched him flip them out. She waited for him to realize that she wasn't inside and call to her, but he didn't. She finally went in after dark, chilly and annoyed. He was already in bed. She lay there for a few minutes listening to him snore and then she crawled into bed beside him. His back was to her. She reached forward and lightly touched the bandage on his neck. For just one second, she thought it felt hot to the touch. Startled she pressed her fingers on the back of his neck. No fever. She stared at the bandage for a moment, and then he rolled over heavily in his sleep, bandage underneath, and pulled her into the circle of his arm, gripping her tightly.

For the next week, Martin left early and came home late. He didn't say much to Hattie one way or another about what was happening at the police station. No amount of gravy, meatloaf or even homemade bread could dent his mood. He grunted his thanks at her for meals and carried them in to eat them in front of the television. He occasionally asked if the kids had called and ignored her responses. The scratch over his eye was healing nicely, but he changed the bandage on his neck every day.

"Mind if I look at that," she asked him one morning, as they were both brushing their teeth. "I just want to make sure it's not getting infected." She reached across the sink to touch the bandage and he jerked away, slamming the mirrored door of his medicine cabinet with his hand.

"Shit, Hattie!" he said, "I'm a grown man. I think I'd know if it's getting infected."

"I'm not going to hurt you Martin," she said. He waved her hand away.

"Damn," he said, "Now you about made me break my hand."

He stomped out of the bathroom.

When Sheriff Martin got the call about Edna Brown's disappearance, his stomach hurt. Just when you think things are going to settle down, he thought. He felt a sudden surge of anger. What the Hell is wrong with this fucking town?

Edna was the manager of the local Dollar Store. She hadn't missed a day of work in twenty-five years. Sarah Reilly, the assistant manager called the Sheriff after she had missed two.

"I thought I'd just screwed up the schedule again," she said on the phone, "But now I'm really worried."

Sheriff Henry and Deputy Smith found no body, no blood, no signs of burglary or violence. The door was unlocked, a window was open. There were a few unwashed dishes in the sink and some damp and mildewed clothes in the washer. It appeared from the state of the house that Edna had simply walked out in the middle of the day and not returned.

Sheriff Henry walked out into the back yard. Clothes hung stiff on the line, yellow with a fine coating of pollen. He walked toward the edge of the property where Edna's yard backed up to the creek. A stand of cane grew thick on the bank. As he approached, he noticed a dark shape moving quickly out of the corner of his eye, darting behind the cane. He felt a chill spread up his back until the hairs on his head stood up. The wound on his neck throbbed.

"Goddamn cat," he whispered hoarsely.

Sheriff Henry came into the laundry room that evening while Hattie was folding socks. He stood in the doorway, blocking the hall light so that she couldn't tell the navy socks from the black. One of the bulbs above her was blown out. She mentally added light bulbs to her shopping list.

"You hear about Edna Brown?" he said. His voice was quiet and careful.

"Yes. Myrtle told me. It seems very odd," Hattie said, then, "You're in my light, Martin."

"It is odd." He didn't move from the doorway. He leaned against the doorframe, filling it.

"Did it look like anything had...you know... happened to her?" Hattie asked, setting a bunch of socks on the washer. She felt very guilty, but at that moment she was more concerned about Martin's stress load than Edna's safety. She had so hoped that solving the case at the church would settle him down.

"There was no sign of violence. The door was unlocked," he answered, "Looks for all the world like she just walked away in the middle of the day. Hard to say when. At least a couple of days."

"That doesn't really sound like Edna," said Hattie. She turned towards him, arms folded on her chest. He stretched up one hand and rested in on the top of the doorframe, blocking her view of the cinderblock basement wall almost entirely.

"No," he agreed, "It doesn't."

"What about Tom?" Hattie asked. Homeless Tom was Edna's son. Who his father was no one but Edna had ever known. Tom wasn't really homeless, Edna kept a room for him. He'd taken to wandering since he was a teenager, camping out by Fish Kill Creek or up on Knobb Mountain when the mood took him, taking on occasional odd jobs and doing handy work. Tom was thirty now.

"He seems unconcerned," said the Sheriff, "Says that his father came back to get her. Makes you wonder, doesn't it?"

"Poor thing," Hattie said, "He's never been quite right, has he? But I don't believe for a minute that he did anything to Edna."

Martin didn't respond, just stood in the doorframe, staring at her.

"Do you have any suspects," she asked after the silence became awkward.

"I don't know that there's anything to suspect," he said, "Her closest kin says she's gone away on purpose. She's not the kind of person that anyone around here would get too fired up about being gone. At least not if everything else was normal. Do you have any ideas what might have happened to her?" Martin swung himself forward in the doorframe a little.

"Why would I have any ideas about it?" she asked.

"Don't know," he said, "Just thought you might."

"I don't know Edna that well," Hattie said, with the distinct feeling that she was walking into a trap that she couldn't see, "I just see her at the Dollar Store now and then."

"I saw your friend there today," Martin said, "So I just thought maybe he knew."

"What are you talking about?" Hattie asked.

"The cat," he said, "I saw that damn cat running through the cane out by the creek. I see that fucking cat every time something strange happens."

"Martin, what's gotten into you?" Hattie said. She stood square in front of him and lifted her chin. She stepped forward as if to push past him.

"Don't leave here, Hattie," he said, "Answer me." He didn't budge.

"You've never been superstitious, Martin," she said, "I know you don't like cats, but this is ridiculous. I really don't know what to say. Do you think the cat made off with her?"

"Do you know why I don't like cats, Hattie?" he asked.

"No, Martin. I do not," Hattie said, "And I'm not particularly interested right now."

She stood very still and looked into his eyes. He leaned forward. She backed away, just a fraction. He reached out and grabbed her arm.

"There's a lot of damned stray cats in this town," he said. He did not loosen his grip on her arm, "Ever had a cat bite Hattie? You can get cat scratch fever."

"Martin, c'mon!" she said. She lightly placed her fingers on the big hand that wrapped her wrist.

"And your cat. Your cat shows up every time there's a dead body or someone disappears. There's something damned eerie about that cat and I know you're feeding it and it's hanging around here all day long. So why don't you explain it to me."

Hattie wrenched her arm out of his hand, "Okay. I'll tell you something," she said, "First of all he's not my cat, and he isn't here every day, no matter what you believe. But you can't be seeing that cat, because he has been with me the times you've claimed to see him. There's no way he's hanging out where bad things are happening. You can believe it or not, but it's true."

"I told you not to bring that cat in here, Hattie!" He said. His voice was shaking, "I told you not to."

"I'm not bringing him in," she said, "I'm not. He's just hangs out in the garden with me. He's not doing anything wrong. I'm not doing anything wrong. This is ridiculous Martin."

Martin let go of her arm. Hattie stepped backwards, involuntarily. She stumbled and found her footing against the washing machine.

He reached up and felt the bandage on his neck for a second.

"You have to leave that cat alone. You have to get it away from here. I can't stand the sight of it. I don't want you to get hurt."

"The cat is not going to hurt me, Martin," said Hattie, "Are you?"

He didn't respond. Just stood there staring at her. Hattie was suddenly aware of the thick cement block walls and drop-down ceiling closing around her.

"Martin," Hattie said quietly, "Can we get Dr. Ford to look at your neck? I think maybe it's infected. Maybe you know...maybe you're not feeling well."

"I don't feel right. That's true," he said, finally, "Maybe I will go in tomorrow." He looked down at his hands, seemed surprised to notice that they were clenched into fists. He uncurled his finger. He turned abruptly and left her alone. She walked over and quietly locked the door. She stood against the washing machine, heart pounding, until she heard him thumping up the stairs.

Hattie lay in bed that night until long after she heard Martin snoring on the living room couch, where she'd found him and covered him with a blanket. She thought about the evening. Martin had always disliked cats, but the distaste he felt for this particular cat was bordering on pathological. He'd never physically restrained her before either. In fact, much to his mother's horror, he'd agreed with Hattie that they wouldn't spank the kids. Sure, they hadn't been getting along terribly well since the kids left, but this was Martin. The man who held her hand through the birth of two children, except when he passed out while Steven was being born. The man who had built her garden bench based on one she'd admired in a magazine. The man who'd stayed up with the kids when they had the stomach flu because Hattie had a hard time with vomit. But the physicality of their encounter wasn't what really frightened her, not even his hatred of the cat. There was something wrong with Martin. When he'd stood there in the laundry room doorway, he hadn't seemed like...Martin. Or he had, but like only the bad impulses of Martin, like Martin with something left out.

In the morning she got up early and went quietly to the kitchen to make biscuits. Martin came into the kitchen after his shower with a fresh bandage on his neck.

"So," she said carefully as she ladled gravy onto his biscuits, "Are you going to see Doctor Ford about your neck today?"

"Yeah," he said, "I'll see what I can do."

"Want me to call and make you an appointment?" she asked.

"No," he said, "I said I'll do it."

She waited until he went outside and then crept to the kitchen window. He was surveying the back yard, hand on his service revolver. He walked to the back and bent down, looking under the rhododendron and the pink azaleas. He made a complete circuit of the yard. She held her breath momentarily. The cat was nowhere to be seen. Martin finally turned and walked back up the driveway.

As soon as she heard Martin's car start and drive down away toward the station, she walked into the back yard. The leaves on her Snow Pearl rhododendron shivered and the cat walked out from under it. She sighed with relief.

The cat walked casually across the grass, absorbing the sunshine into his coat so that for a moment, she saw only a shadow with lemon-yellow eyes. He stretched and put his claws into the hem of her housecoat. She hesitated, then picked him up.

"I guess I'm going to have to find somewhere else for you to be. At least for a little while. I need to think of someone who can keep you inside," she told him as she rubbed his big head under his chin.

"I may have to find somewhere else for me to be too," she whispered.

He closed his eyes and purred. The morning was chilly but the warmth of him radiated from her chest through her whole body. She closed her eyes and buried her nose in his fur. He smelled like grass and sun.

She decided to go and see Myrtle Anderson, the organist from St. Bartholomew's. Myrtle's husband, Edward had told her he would leave her if she got another cat. She had three, which Edward liked to joke was three over his limit. But unlike Martin, Edward was more bark than bite. At any rate, Myrtle might know someone who could take the cat in. If nothing else, she knew she could count on Myrtle to comfort her with coffee and advice.

When she knocked on Myrtle's door, she was surprised to see dark circles under her eyes. Myrtle was still in her pajamas.

"Hey, Myrtle," Hattie said, "Sorry to bother you? I just thought you'd be up because of the kids. I can come back."

"Oh, no problem!" Myrtle said, as she scooped her brown hair up into an elastic band, "I just got up. Edward took the kids this morning. I'm actually really glad you're here. It's all just so upsetting."

"What's upsetting?" Hattie asked, as Myrtle pulled her in and plopped her on the big, worn leather couch.

"Sit right there," Myrtle said, "I need coffee to even talk about it. And you will too, trust me."

Mindy, Myrtle's calico stretched up from the tapestried cushion next to Hattie, hissed and darted under the couch, while Hattie contemplated the mystery.

After a few minutes, Myrtle returned from the kitchen with two steaming coffee cups in the shape of green and turquoise owls. She yawned and sat on the oversized chair, tucking one leg under herself. She shook her head, sipped her coffee, shook her head again.

"It's Alan," Myrtle said, "He tried to kill himself. He's in the hospital. He nearly drowned."

"What? What happened?" Hattie sloshed coffee on her legs.

"Allison called me at 2:30 this morning from the hospital," Myrtle said, "He started practicing piano at two in the afternoon yesterday, apparently mostly fugues. At eight he started playing the Moonlight Sonata over and over. At ten thirty or so, Allison couldn't take it anymore. They got into it. He threw his music stand and ran out the door. You know she lives by the river, right?"

"Oh my God," Hattie said. She found her hand trembling and she looked desperately for a coaster on the coffee table.

"Don't worry about it," Myrtle said, gently taking Hattie's cup, "I'm refinishing it.

"Anyway, he ran out and tried to drown himself. Super weird," Myrtle said, "I don't know what's gotten into him. Allison says he just hasn't been the same person since that thing at the church."

The two women sat quietly for a moment, Myrtle shaking her head.

"He hit his head really hard. Besides, they think now it was partly the infection," Myrtle said, "You know. That place on his neck? It got really bad all of the sudden. He was getting a fever and hallucinations. Allison thought he was getting better after that last round of antibiotics, though."

"Is he going to be okay?" Hattie asked.

"Well, the police fished him out of the river and they took him to the hospital. He's going to live, but I guess he may spend some time in the psych ward," Myrtle answered.

"Myrtle?" said Hattie, "What do you think about that explosion at the church?"

"What do you mean?" Myrtle asked.

"Do you think Father Dingle's story, the one about the demons could be true?"

"Ha!" Myrtle said, "I guess it sure would explain this mess. And maybe this whole damn town. Maybe we are sitting on the edge of Hell."

In the end, Myrtle agreed to take the cat in until she could find a foster home for him. After she finished her coffee, Hattie knew her next step. Before she went home to get the cat, she walked the two blocks to Father Dingle's place. She knocked on the front door. The potted pansies outside the little two-story stone house were withering. A week's worth of papers sat on the stoop. She knew the little man hadn't spoken to anyone in over a week, except maybe Dr. Ford, but she was determined. When he didn't answer at the front door, she walked around the back. She banged even more determinedly there.

She finally heard someone shuffling across the kitchen. The door opened the length of the chain and she saw the glint of Father Dingle's glasses and bald head.

"I'm taking some time off," he said, "I'm so sorry but..."

She found herself putting her hand in the door, "I have to come in Father," she said, "Please. I have to."

When he found that he couldn't shut the door without shutting her hand in it, he relented.

The chain slid out and the door opened. She walked into the stuffy air of the kitchen. He stood there in his plaid flannel housecoat, in slippers. The little wreath of hair that decorated the sides of his bald head stuck out at odd angles. His eyes looked a little glassy. The pills Dr. Ford gave him, thought Hattie. She noted briefly the dishes stacked in the sink, a sour smell emanating from the refrigerator. Brownish bottles lined the sill of the kitchen window and filtered the sun into a dim brown light.

"Would you like to come into the parlor?" he asked.

"No," she said, "The kitchen is just fine."

He swept his fat gray tabby, Cedric, from the chair and patted it. He pulled a chair opposite her.

"Father Dingle?" she asked, "Can you describe the creature that bit Alan on the neck? What do you think it was?"

On her way back to the house, Hattie knew two things for certain. One was that the animal that Martin kept seeing was not the big, black cat. The second was that she had every reason to be afraid. The question was, what should she do about it? She needed time to think.

On her way, she decided to pack a suitcase and go to Myrtle's. Maybe Martin had seen Dr. Ford. Maybe they would take his wound seriously after what happened to Alan. But there was no way she would risk staying there with Martin until she knew for certain he was better one way or another. There was one other thing that troubled her. That was the cat. She would find the cat and take him with her. Martin was certain to shoot him if she didn't. She was nervous, but she felt fairly safe returning to the house. It wasn't even lunchtime yet.

After she packed her suitcase, she dragged it to the kitchen door with her. Now to find the cat. She didn't have far to look. As soon as she opened the door, he sauntered in, tail curved over his back.

"How did you know?" she asked, reaching down to pet him, "We need to get out of here."

He jumped into her arms and she was standing there, nuzzling him, keys in hand, when she heard the sound of tires on the drive. She looked outside. Martin.

"Hello, Hattie," he said as he walked up to the door, "So you don't let the cat in? Is that right?"

Deputy Smith found the kitchen door open. When he stepped into the doorframe, the first thing he saw was Sheriff Henry's back. It took him a moment to process the stance, to understand that Sheriff Henry was holding his wife at gunpoint. Hattie stood pale, shaking, holding an enormous black cat. She was pressed into the corner between the sink and the refrigerator. Strangely, the Deputy could hear the cat purring all the way across the kitchen. Deputy Smith started to tell the Sheriff's wife to remain calm when he saw her slide down into the corner. She was passing out.

At the same moment, he saw the Sheriff's gun slide down with her. He was pointing the gun at her chest. The cat remained with her, sitting against her. The gun was trained on them both. Richard Smith had been shooting with Martin Taylor for too long not to know that moment when he was about to pull the trigger.

"Martin, no!" Deputy Smith called out.

The Sheriff lifted the gun slightly and turned toward Deputy Smith. The deputy had his hand on the gun in his holster.

"Stay out of this, Richard," the Sheriff said.

"I can't, Martin. You know that."

The men stood staring at each other for a moment.

"Please. Put the gun down," the deputy said.

"I'm not going to shoot you, Richard," said the Sheriff, "But the cat has to go. I think it's from Hell."

The Sheriff turned and lifted his gun, training it on the cat, which sat against the unconscious woman's abdomen. Deputy Smith could still hear it purring. Why didn't it run? The Sheriff's finger moved, just a twitch.

"Martin, stop!" the deputy made his decision in an instant, the math a calculation from Hell. He saw the endless stream of nightmares stretching ahead of him even as he pulled the trigger, felt the nausea that he knew would never quite leave his belly. Afterwards, there was no one who didn't agree that he had done the only thing that could be done, including himself, but that didn't make it any better.

The Sheriff went down, thrown onto the white tiles of the kitchen floor by the force of the gunshot. Deputy Smith watched in horror as the blood spread, soaking into the cheerful yellow rag rug by the kitchen sink, turning it apricot on the edges. For a moment the deputy couldn't move. He wasn't sure that he could even breathe. As he stood there, frozen in the moment before he could rouse himself to call an ambulance or check on Hattie, the cat, calmly stretched and yawned, unspooked by the crack of the gunshot. It raised its tail over its back and walked past the deputy and out the door, leaving a trail of bloody red paw prints across the white tile floor, down the kitchen steps and into the green, green grass of the lawn, disappearing like a shadow into the white rhododendron.

The Cat Comes Back

Mr. Wilkerson sat on the porch. Biding his time. A tangle of cobweb hung from one ear, but he did not raise his paw to remove it. The fine threads of spider silk were drifting into his eye on the breeze. His ear quivered. He'd left the burrs where they were and his back quivered with an anxious need to remove them. But he needed to inspire sympathy. Not the emotion he preferred to inspire...but...he did what he had to do. He moved the dead mouse forward, between his paws, so she would see it and understand it was a gift. He'd cleaned most of the blood off it. It was whole, more presentable than his normal offerings, which usually consisted of the head thinly connected to whatever entrails did not appeal to his mood. But he had discovered that many humans had an objection to small piles of intestines. He was a bit hungry, but he could wait. He wasn't nervous. It would work. He felt the vibrations.

Samantha May Alexander stood in the falling twilight of her little back garden with a shovel in her hand. A five-gallon gardenia she'd picked up at Merry Mary's Fine Perennials waited next to her, cheerful, expectant. The hole she'd dug for it was twice as wide and twice as deep as the container the shrub came in, per Mary Holt's instructions. She had her composted manure, humus, and the organic fertilizer Mary recommended. Before she tucked it into the soft blanket of earth, she took a deep breath. The falling night was enticing a lavish, honey-sweet smell from the shrub.

"Mary says gardenias are pollinated by moths. That's why they smell so good at night," she said to a large black cat sitting nearby. "This is the first thing we've planted together."

The cat purred so loudly, Samantha could almost feel the sound vibrating in her own chest. She bent down and rubbed his ears. She picked up an old shoe box that sat next to him. In the dim twilight she shook the contents into the bottom of the hole and set the plant in on top of it. She filled the hole with the manure and humus and patted it in. The cat patted the dirt as well.

"That's that then," Samantha said, "It's time to start over, I guess." Her feelings hovered at an odd, peaceful place between grief and relief.

She rubbed the dirt off her hands. She and the cat sat on the garden bench together, watching the night fall on the little shrub until the moon came out.

The creamy, waxen flowers looked like tiny fluttering ghosts in the evening breeze.

Sam had not expected her stay to turn out like this. She had not expected to plant anything. Plants have roots. She had not planned to put any roots here in Whistlestop. She had not planned to love the wild, overgrown garden or the little yellow house in the center of it. Her whole scheme in moving to Whistlestop had been to sell the house left to her by her Grandma Helen, who had expediently timed her demise just as Sam's relationship of ten years self-destructed. The house materialized like a gift from the fairies. It had been in the family for years, once belonging to her Great-Great Grandma Ida Fox May. She felt very little sentiment for the house based on that fact. She'd never even seen a picture of Ida and whatever happened to her had been lost in the mists of family history. She was curious, of course, but she needed the money from the house to start over.

None of the family still lived in Whistlestop so the little house had suffered years of neglect as a rental. Still, the inspector said the roof was in good shape and the foundation had been shored up. Most of the remaining work Sam could do herself. And she desperately needed a place to go and lick her wounds. Rethink life. She'd packed her bags and left Richard's apartment the day she came home early to find him sleeping peacefully in their bed, naked - with a barista from Java Jill's.

She went to Grandma Helen's funeral, quit her job as a graphic designer, got a few independent consulting gigs and headed for the backwaters. Whistlestop. She would take some time to figure out life, the universe, and everything while she lived rent-free and fixed up the house to sell. Then she could take the money and get her own place. Start over again in a new city.

She was completely unprepared to fall head over heels for the little yellow cottage with the dark green shutters, peeling paint, crooked porch, and overgrown lawn. The butter colored house perched at the top of a hill at the end of Pine Avenue, where it backed up against a few acres of woods. A pink flower or two hovered in the scraggly shrubs in front of the house. The yard, a patchwork of different types of weeds, mowed into a patchwork quilt of soft, mottled greens, sloped gently towards the sidewalk and then suddenly dashed over a steep bank, giving way to a breathless tumble of weeds mixed with sweetheart roses, daylilies, and jonquils. A massive forsythia tilted drunkenly over the concrete stairs that had been cut into the earth for anyone adventurous enough to make the steep ascent. The day Sam moved in, the mist had just burned off, giving way to a hazy blue-gray sky with fingers of sunlight falling through and illuminating the house like a pastel illustration in a children's fairy story. The chaos of weeds and flowers gave the garden the air of a lost paradise.

Not only did the house surprise her, Sam was also unprepared for the cat. She had never had a pet before he showed up on her doorstep looking ragged and hungry. He certainly wasn't a beauty. His left ear was torn, and far from being shiny and beautiful, his scruffy coat was matte black that faded into almost nothing on the ends, covered with burrs, dirt and even a cobweb, as if he'd dug through the earth to appear on her porch.

She couldn't exactly brag about his personality either. As soon as she'd taken pity on him and opened the door, he had suddenly straightened himself, raised his tail in a proud curve over his back and sauntered into the house. The pitiful act he put on was a real con job. He leapt onto the couch kneaded one of the red velvet pillows with his paws and made a bed of it, knocked the other one halfway across the room, and hacked up a piece of mouse, all within the first ten minutes.

She couldn't figure out exactly why she let him stay, except that she had an odd feeling that he came with the house, almost as if her delight in the house had a price and the price was the cat. He had many annoying habits. He was enormous, and he liked to drape himself over her shoulders while she sat at the computer, sometimes licking her ear while she worked. Puffs of his scruffy coat came off on everything she owned. He was so flatulent, she occasionally had to leave the room he was in. He demanded tuna twice a day, generally disdaining the less expensive dry cat food. He refused to be kept indoors if he wanted out, but he howled at doors and windows when he suddenly wanted back inside. He had his own business to take care of, sometimes leaving for the day at five in the morning and demanding to be let in again at midnight.

Still there was something about him that made her feel safe. Something about sleeping with an animal that felt like company, even though she figured, being a cat, he'd probably politely leave the scene if she was attacked or the house was robbed. It had been a long time since Sam had slept alone. More than that, Sam began to develop a strange sensitivity to the cat. Before he'd been there two weeks, she found herself getting up to let him in before he made any kind of sound at all. She found herself asking him whether he wanted canned tuna or chicken, and when she looked at him, she felt that he told her.

If he woke in the night, she woke with him. Sometimes, she swore she could hear mice behind the walls, just the way he could. It was very strange, as though the cat was in her head.

"I'm becoming a crazy old cat lady at twenty-nine," she told him sometimes, "But I'll stop with one cat. You're about all I can handle." She felt he agreed with her.

Before her time with the cat, she had been living with her ex, Richard. She'd been with him ever since her sophomore year of college. They had been together for so long that even her extreme anger at him couldn't overcome all of the loneliness. They'd been inseparable. Now it felt like she'd lost half herself. It was better during the day; she could see him, lying there half covered by the ivory Egyptian cotton sheets she'd saved so long for, the girl with the short blue hair, butterfly tattoo on her shoulder, sleeping under his arm. The mental picture, the nausea, the rage, allowed her to get through the sunlit hours knowing she'd done the right thing.

But at night...at night she remembered his face when she came to pick up her things. How he'd sat on the couch, head in his hands while she packed her clothes. She remembered how he grabbed her arm as she left. When she turned to face him, her resolve almost dissipated. He was pale, trembling, hollow-eyed.

"I love you," he said, "I don't love her. It was just a one-time thing. Please. It will kill me if you go."

She had almost stayed. Almost said she would try. Almost.

Since she'd gone, he had called almost every day. Most times she ignored him.

Only once in the first weeks after she'd moved to Whistlestop did she give in to her weakness and take his call. She was expecting a call from a client that evening. When she heard Richard's voice, she started to sweat.

"Sam," he said, "Don't hang up. Please"

Her stomach flipped, "What do you want to say to me, Richard?" she asked.

"I love you Sam," he said.

"And you prove this by sleeping with a barista from Java Jill's?"

"Sam," he said, "I made a mistake. I love you. I love you."

"But you fucked her?" Sam asked, "Because I don't think that's how it's supposed to work."

"You have to understand, Sam. I've been having a hard time. The stress from my job is killing me," he answered, "It doesn't mean I don't love you."

"Stressed, I understand," she said, "Upset, I understand. Fucking somebody else I do not."

"Can we talk about this?" he said, "I just need to explain. I need you to hear me. I need you back."

"Okay," she said, "Explain."

She hated to admit it but at that moment she had hope. She understood suddenly that it wasn't the end of the world that he'd had sex with someone else. She knew instinctively that there was a magic combination of words, things he could say that would make her go back.

Instead he said, "Sam, you've been gone so much. Your job. It just seems like you're pouring yourself into something that's not us. That's not me. I want things to be the way they were."

"So, this is my fault?" she said, "Is that what you're saying?"

"No Sam," he said, "I'm explaining where my head was. That's all."

"I think you did that," she said. The tears rushed to the back of her throat, but she refused to cry. The hope that she'd hidden even from herself died a sudden and violent death.

"I'm sorry, Richard," she said, "I take a lot of responsibility for things that went wrong between us. I can't take responsibility for that."

"Sam," he said, "That's not what's happening. I'm not blaming you."

"Goodbye, Richard," she said.

"Don't hang up. I can come there! I want to talk this through," she heard him say.

"Don't come here, Richard," she said. She hung up.

The very next day, Sam's neighbor, Miss Edie, knocked at her door. Eden Elizabeth Thompson had lived next door in a small, Victorian cottage of Robin's egg blue with a steep gabled roof and elaborate white trim for all of her eighty-three years. Sam often saw the wiry, gray haired woman yanking weeds in her front garden while wearing a ridiculous floral garden hat and gloves. She hadn't spoken to the old woman since moving day and she was feeling a little guilty about being anti-social. Today, however, hungover from her fight with Richard and exhausted from tossing and turning was not the time she had in mind to rectify the situation.

"Is that your cat?" Miss Edie stood at the top stair, when Sam opened the door. The enormous black cat was spilling from the quilted cushion on the rocking chair. He opened one lemon-yellow eye and yawned.

"Well, not exactly, but sort of. I think it's more like he thinks this is his house," Sam said, "Is he bothering you? He kind of does his own thing." She tried a smile.

"No," said Miss Edie, "I don't mind having a cat next door. I expect he'll keep the squirrels from eating my tulip bulbs. Now, didn't you tell me you were related to Ida Fox May? The woman that used to live here so long ago?"

"Yes," said Sam, wondered at the abrupt turn in the conversation, "She was my great-great grandmother. But I don't know much about her. Sorry."

Miss Edie looked at the cat and back at Sam, "Sugar or oatmeal?" she asked.

"Beg your pardon?" Sam said.

"Cookies," said Miss Edie, "Sugar or oatmeal?"

"Umm...sugar?" Sam said.

"Fine," said Miss Edie, "You put the kettle on. I'll be right back. I have something for you."

Miss Edie came back with an old cool whip container in one blue-veined hand and what appeared to be a small leather book in the other.

"Have a seat," Sam said, waving Miss Edie to the couch and moving to turn the red velvet pillow over. Too late, she realized it was covered in cat hair on both sides.

"Oh, let's have our tea at the kitchen table," Miss Edie said, "I always think it's friendlier."

And less hairy, thought Sam. She glared at the cat who'd sauntered in when she opened the door for her neighbor. He appeared totally unconcerned.

Miss Edie walked in the kitchen where the sun was coming through the big, square windows and puddling on the faded linoleum floor, "I'm glad you took those old blinds down. I wouldn't put up curtains if I were you. It's plenty private with the fence and the blackberry hedge. Besides, who gets up to nonsense in the kitchen they don't want the neighbors to see?"

Sam laughed, "Not me," she said, "I don't have anyone to get up to nonsense with. Just me and the cat."

Miss Edie plunked the cool whip container and the leather book on the scuffed pine table.

"You need to sand this and re-stain it," she said, "But it's a nice table. It ought to be a nice golden color when you're done. It'll be too pretty for a tablecloth with all those knots."

"Thanks," Sam said. She wondered how long Miss Edie would be there and whether she could find a graceful way to shoo the old lady out before she made room by room suggestions of paint colors and window treatments. She wasn't terribly excited when she saw that the book on the table was a photo album.

"Aha!" said Sam, "Pictures." She tried to look interested.

"I'm not here to make you look through boring pictures of kids and grandkids. For goodness sakes," Miss Edie said, "For one thing, I don't have kids or grandkids, and I'm not especially fond of either of my nephews. My niece isn't awful, but she's not much to look at, truth be told. Sit down over here next to me. There's something in here you'll be real interested in."

Sam sat obediently at the table. She was just stuffing a sugar cookie into her mouth when Miss Edie opened the photo album. The cat walked onto the table and stood over the album too.

Sam tried in vain to push him off the table while crumbs fell everywhere, "Goodness," she told him, "Get your old cat butt off the table." He shifted just out of Sam's reach.

Miss Edie laughed, "Oh, leave him be. He might be as interested in this as you are."

"Look here," Miss Edie said pointing to an old yellowed, black and white photo on the left-hand side of the album. A woman in a white ankle length dress, with a mass of black hair piled on her head, tendrils escaping here and there looked back at Sam. The woman was smiling, seated in a big wicker chair, leaning gracefully on the arm, her chin in her hand. There spread out like an ink stain across the woman's dress was a huge, black cat.

"That," Miss Edie said, "Is your great-great grandma Ida. And her cat."

The cat sat on the table washing his paws.

"Looks a lot like that one," Miss Edie said, pointing at him, "Doesn't it?"

Miss Edie looked expectantly up at Sam, who was still trying to choke down the cookie, so she could respond politely.

"He does," she said, spitting crumbs, "He looks an awful lot like great-great grandma's cat."

Miss Edie took the yellowing photo out of the album and turned it over. In a spidery hand, someone had written Ida and Mr. Wilkerson, 1918.

"That's the cat's name?" asked Sam, "Mr. Wilkerson?"

The cat purred. "I suppose that was one of your illustrious ancestors?" Sam asked him.

"I guess you're, like, Mr. Wilkerson the third, or the fourth," Sam said.

Miss Edie shrugged, "Who knows? They say cats have nine lives."

Sam laughed, "I'm pretty sure they use up those lives in a pretty short time." The cat walked over and curled up on her shoulders. Sam rubbed his ears.

"So, you're the great-great-great grandchild of old man Wilkerson," she said, "I guess we know why you think this house belongs to you."

Miss Edie handed the photo to Sam. "Look at that. You look an awful lot like Ida May," she said, "Except she was a small woman. You're built slender like she was but taller."

"I've never seen a picture of her before," Sam said, turning the photo over in her hand, "No one in my family says much about her."

"Really?" Miss Edie said, "People here still talk about Ida. She made quite an impact on the town."

"What do you mean?" asked Sam.

"The people around here used to claim she was a witch," Miss Edie said, "At some point, some of the church people ran her out of town. Or she disappeared. Everyone has an opinion."

"A witch?" Sam asked, "When was that? I thought witch trials went out in the sixteen hundreds."

"I don't know that witch trials ever really went out of style," Miss Edie responded, "People are always looking for someone to torment and blame things on. Lordy, I wish I knew why. Anyhow, whatever it was that happened, happened in the late twenties."

"So, people thought my great-great grandmother was a witch?" Sam asked, "For real? What the heck? Why didn't anyone ever tell me?"

"Ida's daughter, your great-grandmother, left with her family in the middle of the night shortly after Ida disappeared. I reckon they were afraid. They were being threatened. They couldn't sell Ida's house. It fell into disrepair for a while, then I guess the family started renting it out through an attorney or a real estate company. I can't say when I've seen anyone from your family back in Whistlestop until you arrived."

"Does everyone in town know all this information but me?" Sam asked.

"You have to understand. My grandmother and Ida were great friends. My grandmother lived right next door, where I live now. They raised their kids together. Mamaw Maggie would tell me all about her, only it had to be when my mama couldn't hear. Mama didn't like the tales she told about Ida."

"Why not?" asked Sam.

The old lady laughed, "My mama was nothing if not Jesus' right hand woman. If those church doors were open, we were there. She didn't hold with talking about witches and superstitions. She also didn't approve of Mamaw Maggie, who didn't have near as much use for the church. So, when her mother-in-law started up talking about Ida being a witch and a good one at that, Mama shut it down."

"Your grandmother thought Ida was a good witch?" Sam said, "She surely wasn't serious. She must have been telling you stories to entertain you."

"Mamaw Maggie was dead serious about Ida," Miss Edie said, "That's why she quit going over to church. She said if God wanted her to disapprove of one of the best women she'd ever known and take up for the wicked she was done. And she never did go back."

"Why did she think Ida was a witch?" asked Sam.

"She told me that Ida was always helping people, healing them, making love potions. Once, Mamaw told me she got a stillborn baby to breathe. That baby was Maggie's third son, my father."

"If she was helping people why did they run her out of town?" Sam asked. She decided to let the story of the baby pass without response. She had no idea how serious Miss Edie was about it.

"Same thing that happens to too many women," Miss Edie said, "She was still a beautiful woman after she was widowed. Her next-door neighbor, man named Bill Cuthbert, looked at her with 'lust in his heart' as they say at church, and when she rebuffed him, he decided to have his revenge. He started agitating around town. Telling people that she was a witch. That she had to be working with the devil."

"And they just ran her off..." Sam said, "Do you think...do you think they killed her? That might explain why no one ever heard from her again. And why my family doesn't want to talk about it."

"Well," said Miss Edie, "The story goes – and it's a hard one to believe – that Bill Cuthbert and his wife Myrna got a mob together. They chased her to the judge's house. What they planned to do with her, I don't know. At any rate, once they got there, Bill threatened her and in the heat of the moment, she turned him into a snake. As soon as it happened, her cat," here Miss Edie paused and pointed at the cat on the table, "killed him by shaking him. Then the cat and Ida and the little dead snake disappeared. Just like that."

"Like disappeared in a puff of smoke?" Sam asked.

"Pretty much," Miss Edie said. She sipped her tea.

"You can't believe that!" Sam said, "Don't you think it's more likely that she was murdered."

"Of course, anything else is more likely than that," Miss Edie responded, "But that's what my grandmother believed until the day she died."

"What do you think?" Sam asked her.

"Oh," Miss Edie said, "I don't know. I always thought the judge got her out the back door and out of town. That maybe she was able to contact her daughter. Though talking to you, it seems strange that the family lost track of her after they moved away."

"What about Bill," Sam asked, "The man she supposedly killed? Did the judge spirit him away too?"

"His name is on Myrna's tombstone in the churchyard," Miss Edie said, "But I've always been told the only body that lies there is hers."

"This is all very weird," Sam said.

"True," said Miss Edie, "It's probably all nonsense. But I thought you might find it interesting."

Sam shook her head, "Do you mind if I make a copy of this photo?" she asked.

"Of course not," Miss Edie said, "You can keep it if you like and give me a copy." She pushed back her chair and stood up, "There's more cookies. Just run the empty container back when you're finished."

"Thanks," Sam said.

"I'll let myself out," Miss Edie said as she walked to the kitchen door, "Just one more thing. Who on earth were you arguing with last night?"

Sam blushed, "My ex."

"Well," Miss Edie said, "If you're going to have arguments with the windows open and interrupt my sleep, you could at least do the courtesy of putting him on speaker-phone, so I can hear both sides of the argument."

"Yeah," Sam said, "Sorry."

"It's okay," said Miss Edie, "Stick to your guns. If he can't keep it in his pants, you don't need him."

Sam blushed, "I think you got plenty of information from one side of the conversation."

"I've lived by myself my entire life," Miss Edie said, "You don't need him. Too many women think they can't get by without a man."

"I'll keep it in mind," Sam said.

Far from being annoyed by Miss Edie, Sam found herself relying on the old lady. She had never gardened before. Her original thought was simply to cut down the plants around the house and yard, to simply clear the property before selling it, but somehow when she saw that pink flower in the front sticking a spindly arm waving its delicate pink flower like an offering, she felt she had to save it. Miss Edie was a great aid in helping her sort the weeds from the perennials. She learned that the pink flowered shrub in the front was an azalea.

"Look at that!" Miss Edie said when they cleared away the weeds and crab grass at its feet, "I'll be! That thing looks like it might have been here since Ida's day, big as the trunk is. Hard to believe it made it. Their roots don't like to compete. Amazing. It looks a little rangy, but we might save it yet."

Sam was strangely excited. In fact, Mr. Wilkerson seemed excited by it too. After Miss Edie went back to her house for some fertilizer, the cat rubbed against

Sam's legs as she touched the glossy green leaves. It was then, for the first time, that the cat put a word into her head. She couldn't explain it, except to say that it happened. She felt the word travel from the cat's head up her leg and into her head. From there, it came out her lips quite naturally.

She whispered it to the bush she held in her hand and she could have sworn she felt it tremble. A strange energy moved from the cat through her body and into the plant. She stumbled backwards.

Miss Edie came back, and they fertilized the plant. By the next morning, the azalea had put on at least twice as many full-sized green leaves and blooms as it had the day before. The old lady looked from the bush to Sam.

"I never have seen a bush use fertilizer that fast," she said.

Sam shrugged. By the following week, the old azalea was covered in leaves and blooms. Miss Edie shook her head at it but kept her peace.

It was not the last time the cat helped her with the garden. Miss Edie helped Sam clear the spot where Ida's herb garden had been. The cat gave her a word one day that had small sprigs of rosemary and mint sprouting up from the earth by the next day.

"Did you go by Merry Mary's?" Miss Edie asked. She looked at the tender little shoots of plants springing from the ground and then back to Sam and Mr. Wilkerson.

"Ummm..." Sam said. Miss Edie bent over the fresh new plants, muttering to herself. Finally, she looked up at Sam, wide-eyed.

"Be careful, girl," said Miss Edie, "Keep it to yourself."

After that, Miss Edie answered her questions about gardening without asking any. Sometimes she asked Sam to come over to help at her own house. She inevitably went inside and stayed long enough for Ida's granddaughter and the cat to do what they needed to do. Within a few weeks, Mamaw Maggie's old crabapple tree had put on new branches and fresh green leaves. Miss Edie's asparagus had spread a few extra feet and her roses were entirely cured of mildew in spite of the humidity that spring. Miss Edie became quite fond of Sam and Mr. Wilkerson.

One morning, when Miss Edie didn't drop by for her usual cup of tea, Sam decided to go and check on her. The cat ran ahead, straight into the backyard of the little blue cottage.

"Miss Edie!" Sam called.

She heard a scrabbling by the hydrangeas. She and Mr. Wilkerson ran to the sound to find Miss Edie lying on the grass. Her mouth opened and shut, but no words came out.

"Oh my god!" Sam said, "Miss Edie! Miss Edie's having a heart attack or a stroke!"

"Miss Edie," she patted the old woman's cheek, "I'll be right back! I'm going to get my phone!"

She jumped and nearly tripped over Mr. Wilkerson, "Not now buddy! I need my phone."

He pushed against her hard, and she heard the word. She stopped. Her skin tingled. She turned back to the old woman on the ground. Bent down. Held her hand. The word came from her lips. The old woman trembled from head to foot. For a moment, Sam thought she was dying. Then Miss Edie sat up and rubbed her temples.

"For goodness sakes girl!" she said, "You have Ida's gift."

"I didn't do it by myself," said Sam, "Really, it's him."

The cat climbed up into Miss Edie's lap.

"For goodness sakes!" Miss Edie said again.

"I'm going to call an ambulance," Sam said.

"No need for that," Miss Edie said, "I haven't felt this good for ten years."

Later that night, Sam sat at her window looking at the stars. It was the same window, the same stars that Great-Great Grandmother Ida knew. Sam could almost feel her there.

"This is some weird shit, Ida," Sam said. A velvet breeze, with a sweet, lush scent brushed her face, "What am I supposed to do about this?"

The breeze didn't answer her. It brushed her face and lifted tendrils of hair off her neck. She felt a strange chill even though the night was warm. She crawled back into bed and pulled up the quilt. Mr. Wilkerson walked up the bed and placed himself between her legs, burrowing into the quilt. He was purring. A sleepy warmth crawled through her from the cat to her head and she slept. The sweet-scented breeze swept into the window and she dreamed of gardens at the edge of the world, where Ida walked in a white gown.

It was in the middle of the night that Richard came. Even before Sam heard the banging on the door, the cat was patting her on the face. She sat up, sweet dreams disintegrating. Her first instinct was fear, then she heard his voice.

"Sam, let me in! It's me! Richard."

Sam rose and threw the quilt around her white nightgown.

She went to the door, "Go away Richard! You'll wake up the neighbors. I told you not to come here."

"I had to, Sam. Had to come. Please," he banged on the door again, "Just talk to me. Ten minutes."

"Oh, for heaven's sake!" Sam opened the door and Richard almost fell into the room, "The only reason I'm letting you in here is because I don't want you to worry Miss Edie. Come in and shut up."

Richard came in and tried to hug Sam. She pushed him away.

"Please. Just go sit on the couch. I'll make some tea."

He flung himself on the couch and folded his arms across his chest. Sam noticed that Mr. Wilkerson sat on the coffee table in front of him, staring.

"What's with the creepy animal?" he asked, "Good God, he looks like a witch's cat. Come here buddy." Richard held out his hand. The cat sat stone still. Richard shrugged.

"Not very friendly, is he?"

"He sort of showed up," Sam said from the kitchen, "I think you might be a little creepier than he is right now, since he lives here, and you don't, and you showed up in the middle of the damn night. Good God! You nearly gave me a heart attack."

"Can you put him out?" Richard asked, "I'm not crazy about him."

"No, I cannot put him out of his own house," Sam said, "And you will not be here long enough to worry about."

Sam sat down across from Richard and pushed a cup of tea at him.

"It has honey instead of sugar. Just the way you like it," she said, "Now, why don't you have the tea, tell me what you need to say, and then you can be on your way."

"The thing is, Sam. It's this," Richard swept his hand across the room, including her in the scope of his gesture, "You making tea. You making breakfast. Cooking dinner together. Hanging out at Beards and Beers, going to the Quail Egg on Saturday nights. I loved doing all those things with you. I didn't realize how much I would miss you."

"Then you shouldn't have fucked the woman from the coffee shop."

"Sam," he leaned forward and put his hand on her knee, "We wouldn't be the first couple who got past an infidelity."

"Let me ask you something," she said, "Was that the first time? Because there was something about the way she was sleeping next to you. It was too familiar."

He hesitated for just a second too long, "Of course."

Sam stood up, "Out. Seriously. You could at least do me the courtesy of telling me the truth. Out."

Richard stood up, leaned over the coffee table and grabbed her arm. His eyes were wide, and his fingers hurt her wrists. She could feel his thumb pressing a bruise into her arm.

"Sam. I will not leave without you!" he said. He pulled her towards him, "I won't! I love you! I didn't know how much until you left!"

Sam felt she was smothering. It was more than his body weight. The weight of the decade she'd spent with him crushed her chest. Wasted time. Boundaries. Lies. She tried to wrench her hand back from him, but he pulled her against him roughly wrapping his arm around her waist, his lips on her neck.

"I love you so much," he was crying, "I can't let you go."

The cat was at her feet and the word was at her lips before she knew quite what she was doing.

Richard started back and made a shriek, like he'd been stung by a bee, but the noise morphed into a squeak. His hands shot out and his fingers stretched, curving, clawlike. His nose pulled forward and he pawed it squealing. Whiskers sprouted from the sides. His ears stretched upward and grew pointed. While this was happening, he was becoming smaller and smaller. He jumped up as if in pain and that's when Sam saw the tail sprouting from his back side. His eyes shrunk to two round dots and then he fell to the floor. She couldn't quite figure out how he'd disappeared. Then she saw it. A small dark rat, blinking back at her.

Sam's hands flew to her face and she leaned down, trying to figure out what she'd done, whether she could fix it. But before she could do anything, the cat leapt forward, shaking the rat in his mouth. One shake. Two. Three and the rat ceased moving.

"Oh, Mr. Wilkerson," Sam said. She picked him up and held him to her chest. He still had the rat in his mouth, "Naughty, naughty Mr. Wilkerson."